DESIRE

SERIES READING ORDER

Brightest Kind of Darkness Series

ETHAN *
BRIGHTEST KIND OF DARKNESS
LUCID
DESTINY
DESIRE
AWAKEN

*ETHAN is a prequel that delves deeper into Ethan's background.
It's best read **after** BRIGHTEST KIND OF DARKNESS.

The Brightest Kind of Darkness series is best suited for
readers 16+.

GLOSSARY OF TERMS

A list of terms to help you get reacquainted with the BKoD world.

Celestial realm – Heaven

Mortal realm – Earth

Under realm - Hell

Veil - a safety zone around the Mortal realm where angels constantly fight demons to keep them from breaking through the veil and entering the Mortal realm

Inferi - a demon who followed Lucifer when he was cast from the Celestial realm, ie a Lucifer demon

Inferni - plural of Inferi

Furia - a lower demon created if a Corvus kills a human who is fully possessed (corrupted) by an Inferi.

Furiae - plural of Furia

Corvus - a human who has been chosen to host a piece of the Master Corvus ' spirit. The Corvus' sole purpose is to maintain balance between good and evil in the Mortal realm by fighting demons who possess humans. The Corvus expels the demon from the human, sending it back to Under (if it's a Inferi demon) or killing it for good (if it's a Furia demon).

Master Corvus - a powerful spirit who creates Corvus.

Order - A secret organization that oversees finding newly formed Corvus and assigning a Paladin to help the human adjust to the physical and mental changes he/ she will experience as a Corvus.

Paladin - a human , with his/ her own special ability, who has dedicated his/ her life to the Order to help the Corvus. A Paladin gives the Corvus moral support through a human connection who understands their purpose. The Paladin's goal is to help the Corvus stay grounded to the human world so that the Corvus won't go dark from the demonic evil he/ she has to fight on a constant basis.

Archangel – The highest-ranking angel

CHAPTER 1

NARA

"*A*re you an angel, Nara?"

Ethan's deep blue eyes search mine, hard. I'm not sure what he hopes to find. Deception? Amusement? Confusion? Most definitely that last one.

"I'm not an angel." The conversation I'd just had with Michael downstairs before the archangel vanished flashes through my mind. I hold Ethan's gaze for another beat, then shrug. Michael pretty much told me that the raven spirit inside Ethan, his Corvus, has lost sight of who he is...and Michael chose me to lead the spirit back to the truth about himself. "Michael says I need to study the map more before we burn it," I say, turning down the hall toward my room.

"Michael?" Ethan falls into step behind me. "As in the archangel who kicked Lucifer out of heaven? He's the blond man who's been popping up and talking to people in our lives?"

"The one and only," I say over my shoulder and enter my room. "At least now he's no longer a mystery.'"

"Why did he say we should study the map?"

"He wants to make sure we stay on track. The map must be important somehow."

Ethan frowns as I pull the map out of my metal trashcan now sitting in the middle of my room. He'd folded and shoved the map in it, ready for me to torch the paper once I returned with the matches. "On track to what?"

I shake my head and spread the map back out on my desk. "My guess is it has something to do with my connection to ravens and the Corvus."

Excitement fills his expression. "So he told you what your role is?"

"Just that I'm supposed to help the Corvus," I say, then swing my attention to the paper. "Somehow this map plays a part. Why else would he tell me to study it more before I destroy it?"

Technically, there's just *one* Corvus that Michael asked me to help. But Ethan has only just started to accept the dark and dangerous mystical aspects of the Corvus spirit within him. He has already refused to believe what Fate said to me earlier: that Ethan isn't just any Corvus, he's the Master Corvus—the main spirit responsible for creating *all* Corvus. Not that I blame him for his skepticism of Fate. Any dealings I've had with the vengeful, smoky entity in the past have always turned into Fate trying to take what he wanted from me, no matter the cost.

Michael confirmed Fate's motive for telling me the true identity of the Corvus inside Ethan was to protect his own hide from the Master Corvus' wrath. The powerful raven spirit had already threatened Fate once for attacking me in Ethan's dream world. And now Fate wants me to keep the Master Corvus in line. Ironic how Fate expects me to have a conscience when he doesn't.

Fate is the least of my worries. Michael's revelation about Ethan has left me wondering—What is the best way to tell

Ethan that the Corvus inside him has forgotten the critical role *he* plays in ridding our world of the demons possessing humans? Without the Master Corvus' involvement, if another Corvus dies while trying to save a possessed person from a demon, no new Corvus will be created, and the balance between Corvus and Inferni (Lucifer's demons) and Furiae (lower demons) would skew strongly in the demons' favor. I want to tell Ethan that Michael confirmed Fate's statement about the Master Corvus, but right now, he's in major denial mode—most likely bolstered by his Corvus' fierce and adamant refusal to believe. He's too wound up to accept the truth. For now.

"Why didn't Michael talk to me too?" Ethan's disgruntled question filters through my conflicted thoughts as I push the wrinkles out of the map. I mumble about differing vibrational levels and try to concentrate on the red marks I'd made earlier with the feather tattoo I'd peeled off my shoulder blade.

Um, yeah…if you had asked me back in October if tattoos could turn into real objects, I'd have laughed in your face. Then again, that was before I'd met Ethan and learned that Fate, demons, and angels actually exist and aren't just fictional characters created to keep us in line.

I might dream my next day every night when I fall asleep —well, I still would if the ring I wear to keep demons from trying to possess me didn't block my dreams now—but supernatural tattoos? Yep, they exist. They do if you're intimately connected to a Corvus. Whereas the sword tattoo running diagonally down Ethan's back can turn into a kickass demon-obliterating weapon, I just have a white feather on my right shoulder blade.

His sword can dispatch demons back to Under.

My feather can apparently plot points on a map.

Woohoo, I'm *so* badass.

I'm still fuzzy how my feather went from sitting in my hand to a pen with red ink. All I remember is feeling compelled to douse the bright spots flickering in my eyes every time I stared at the world map on my desk. Touching each spot with the feather pen worked, and before I knew it, I'd mapped out all the Corvus' locations across the world. I'm not certain I could repeat the process again; the whole experience felt very out-of-body. And I have no clue why the top of my feather turned black after that.

"What did you say, Nara? You mumbled something."

"Huh?" I pull out of my musings, my thoughts still whirling.

Ethan's brow creases with worry. "Are you okay?"

"Yeah, just thinking." *How I have no idea what I'm looking for on this map. Or how I'm supposed to help you. Michael has far more faith in me than I do.*

"Michael has interacted with many people in our lives, keeping our paths together. He's even talked to you a few times. Why hasn't he ever spoken to me?"

"While we were talking about the raven book she created for Michael, Madeline told me that angels can't talk to Corvus. Something about the Corvus spirit existing at a higher vibrational level."

Ethan grunts his frustration and rubs his jaw. "Carrying around a highly evolved raven spirit seems so surreal. Half the time I feel like I'm going to wake up in a sleep-drool puddle next to a raven-inspired graphic novel I fell asleep reading."

"Oh, so the main character in this hypothetical graphic-novel-inspired dream finally gets the girl all to himself?" I raise an eyebrow and tilt my head toward my rumpled bedcovers.

Ethan smiles and runs his knuckles along the side of my throat, his blue eyes warm as they slide over my face. "For that alone, I'm very, very glad this is no dream, Sunshine." Pulling me close, he presses his lips to mine, then nods to the map. "Okay, so Michael thinks what you've mapped here is important. Did he give any idea as to what you're looking for?"

I stare at the purple marks. "These marks represent me tracking unusual events—like power grid surges, a massive sink hole, or a train derailment—that have coincided closely with natural disasters such as hurricanes, tornados, earthquakes, etc. Cross-referencing those events provides an area where potential cracks might form in the veil between our Mortal realm and the Under realm. And those cracks are where Madeline said demons can break through." I slide my finger across the red dots I'd added using the feather. "You confirmed these are Corvus all over the world. I know there's something I'm supposed to see here—" The song "Perfect Strangers" by Deep Purple blasting from my phone cuts me off.

When Ethan's eyebrows shoot up at the old song, I snicker and walk over to grab my phone off my nightstand. "Once my dad and I have caught up on the last decade he missed from my life, I'll change it."

Ethan shakes his head as I put the phone to my ear. "Hey, Dad. What's up?"

"I'm about fifteen minutes away. I hope I didn't wake you, but I decided I wasn't going to miss another holiday with my daughter. I plan to stay in Blue Ridge for a few days, then head back to D.C. after Christmas. I know your mom's not around, so I thought I'd swing by."

"You'll be here in fifteen minutes? I just woke up." I gulp, my gaze jerking to Ethan's in panic.

"Why do you sound surprised? Didn't you already dream this?" my father asks.

"Well, I didn't get much sleep last night. Kind of tossed

and turned." I bite my lip to keep from laughing when Ethan pauses in the process of putting his shirt on to flash me a wicked smile, fully confident in his ability to keep me awake most of the night. "How'd you know Mom's not here?"

"I may have given up my ability to see my next day when I faced down Fate, but I still have my government connections, Nari. It was easy enough to find out that your mom flew out on Saturday and that she'll be returning on Monday. I thought we could spend the morning discussing how best to approach her about why I left."

Ethan moves to my side and lifts my free hand, pressing a kiss to my knuckles. I don't want him to go, so I pout at him and answer my father. "Okay, see you soon."

Once I hang up, Ethan gestures to the map. "Looks like we've got a lot less time to study that now."

"I can always destroy it later."

When he frowns, my shoulders sag. Waiting isn't an option. If demons got a hold of this map, they'd know every single Corvus' location. And right now there's at least one demon who'll be sniffing around my house for a book he thinks I still have the second he finds himself another body to inhabit. Turning to the map once more, Ethan and I spend the next few precious minutes we have alone together studying it one last time, hoping for some kind of inspiration to strike.

Ethan finally glances at me and shakes his head. "I've got nothing."

A knot of failure curls in my belly, especially since I have no idea if I can replicate the map again. "Me either." With a sigh of frustration, I begin to fold the map up once more.

While we watch the folded paper quickly burn to ash in my trashcan, Ethan stands behind me and wraps his arms around my waist.

"You still have Freddie's raven book. Fate said it's important. Why don't we try looking over it? Maybe with both of us reading through it, something will click."

I nod, appreciating that he seems to know how bereft I feel without me saying a word. "It's in a safe place for now, buried next to Freddie's gravestone. I'll get it later so we can have time to look through it."

Ethan's hold on me tightens, his warmth surrounding me as he murmurs against my ear, "I might have to leave for now, but I'm glad I have your forever kiss, because I'm never letting you go."

Butterflies explode in my stomach, unraveling the knot. I rest my head against his shoulder and glance up at him, smiling. "I love you too. Now go before my dad arrives to see you leaving just as the sun is rising. That would *not* go over well."

"He'll never see me." Ethan cast an arrogant smile my way before leaving my room in a blur. I snort when I hear the front door shut behind him a split second later. Good to know his Corvus speed can come in handy in other ways too.

Once the map is nothing but black ash, I walk over to my window and open it to let the room air out. Patch is waiting on the ledge outside, but the second the raven gets a whiff of the smoke, he flies away with an annoyed *gronk, gronk.* "Aw, don't go away mad," I call after him while I dump the ashes out my window, but I know it's for the best.

My father might not know about the Corvus history in our world, but with my help he did share Ethan's nightmares, which is how he was able to finally see and confront Fate, so he's very aware of what Ethan's sword can do—at least in a dream world. He doesn't know that the sword came from a tattoo on Ethan's back or that the demon that Ethan killed in that dream wasn't just horrific nightmare imagery, but a memory of Ethan's. And since I'm not sure if my dad saw the raven yin-yang symbol on the sword, the last thing I want him to see is a raven with a white spot of feathers around its eye hanging around outside my window. No need to give him too many dots to connect.

This constant "keeping secrets" thing is for the birds. I chuckle at my own internal pun, then quickly turn to get dressed and straighten up before my dad arrives.

The house smells like brewing coffee by the time my father knocks. Houdini does his normal alert bark and puts himself between me and the front door. But the moment I pull it open, he gives my dad a quick you-pass-the-test sniff, then bolts for the family of rabbits currently living in a burrow under the nativity scene in our front yard.

"Houdini!" I call sharply. He skids to a halt, kicking up tufts of snow and turns his head my way, giving me a pleading look that totally says, *But I just wanna chase them. C'mon, can't I? Just a little.* "Leave them alone and do your business."

After he barks once at the strange car parked in front of the house, then schleps off to sniff for a spot among the trampled down snow, my dad shifts his green eyes back to me, dark eyebrows raised in amusement. "Looks like you've got that big guy well in hand."

I shrug and pull the door wide for him. "He listens to Ethan better than me."

My father's mouth presses slightly at the mention of Ethan's name, but he doesn't say anything. Taking off his fedora hat, he sniffs the air once he steps inside and grins. "Bless you, Nari. You made coffee."

I laugh and wait until Houdini trots back inside. The second my dog enters, he instantly seeks my dad's location. Finding him setting his trench coat and hat on a stool next to the island, he immediately walks up to my dad and sits down, waiting to be patted.

"You're a big lug, aren't you?" Dad says rubbing Houdini's head.

I'm kind of taken aback at how Houdini acts around my father. Usually he'll stick to my backside like my shadow until he feels he can trust the person, but he's not like that with my dad. For whatever reason, he's giving him instant trust, which makes me smile. "He likes you."

My dad glances up and continues to pet Houdini. "I take it your mom's able to tolerate him with her allergies?"

"So long as I vacuum a couple times a week."

He nods his understanding. "I've always wanted a dog, but worked such long hours it wouldn't have been fair to get one."

I tilt my head and watch my dad get down on one knee to rub Houdini's jowls, then scrub his fur on his neck. He looks like he genuinely enjoys playing with my dog. Who knew they'd take to each other so quickly.

I walk into the kitchen and take down a couple of mugs from the cabinet. My dad and I seem to be dancing around the real reason he's here. It's like neither one of us wants to have to discuss the fact that Mom thinks he abandoned us.

Fate.

Ugh, if the human race didn't need that narcissistic being, I'd have let Ethan's Corvus slice the vengeful entity to shreds with his sword for threatening my father's life in Ethan's dream world. His shadowy, merciless ways have been the biggest wedge in our family for far too long. But now that my dad can't see the future in his dreams any more, he can't meddle in other people's fates, so Fate's no longer interested in making his life a living hell.

I pour both mugs full of black coffee, my mind wandering. How do I tell my mother that dad left to protect us from a supernatural force? Because to do so, I'll have to tell her I've kept my ability from her too. Would Mom see that revelation as a double betrayal? My stomach churns just thinking about it.

"You okay, Nari?"

I smile and hand him his cup of coffee. "I'm good." When I sit down on the stool next to him at the island, he nods to my cup and takes a sip from his.

"You drink it black? Unusual for your age."

"Sometimes." I take a couple of sips, then shudder and grimace. "Okay, never, but today I need full strength to fuel me if we're going to brainstorm how to approach Mom."

My father's expression turns serious and he sets his cup down. "You're nervous."

I nod. "I just don't know how she's going to take it."

He stares into my eyes, understanding finally reflecting in his own. "You're worried she'll blame you somehow, aren't you?" Palming the top of my head, he lowers his own until our gazes meet. "She could never blame you, Nari. You're her everything. Always have been."

I want to tell him just how *not* well she took his leaving us when he releases me to clasp his mug. But it feels too private. Like he shouldn't know how much mental anguish my mother went through—the years of depression and therapy it took to get over thinking her husband just up and abandoned her. I think that kind of detail should come from her…if she ever decides to share it.

"I do think showing her the videos is a good idea, but I'd like to be there when you do," my dad says, holding his cup up.

I shake my head in fast jerks. "No, Dad. I have to ease her into—"

The sound of the garage door opening yanks my attention to the back door. Panic ramps my heart. "Crap. She's home early." *Probably to shop for a dang Christmas tree with David.*

10

My father stands, appearing relaxed and unruffled while I grab the coffee cups and dump them in the sink. "We have to talk eventually," he says calmly.

"But not this way. You can't just shock her like this." I say in a fast huff, grabbing up his coat and hat and shoving them in his arms. Nodding toward the stairs, I say, "Please go upstairs to my room and give me a chance to talk to her first."

"Inara…" he begins, a parental look settling on his face.

A car door slams outside and the garage door starts to shut.

My palms tingle, sweat seeping to the surface. My breathing turns labored. "Please, Dad. Do this for me."

"Very well." He sighs and sets his hat on his head, then heads up the stairs.

"I'll call you down in a few minutes," I quietly call after him before he disappears around the corner.

"Hi, Mom," I say, my voice pitched higher than usual. Clearing my throat, I quickly follow up. "You're home early. Did something go wrong with your meeting?"

She nods and unwinds her scarf from her neck. "The person I was supposed to meet with came down with the flu. Apparently it's spreading like the plague through that office and no one bothered to tell me before I flew out there." Walking over to the living room window, she peers outside and unbuttons her coat. "Who's car is sitting outside our house? Did Ethan get a different car?" Turning her light blue eyes my way, she frowns. "He's not upstairs is he, Inara?"

"No." I shake my head and move into the living room. "Actually, the car is something I'd like to talk to you about."

Confusion reflects on my mother's face. "Whose car is it?"

"Well, it's…" I pause and shove my hands deep in my

jeans' back pockets, unsure what to say next. I don't even know where to start.

Worry creases my mom's forehead and she steps forward to clasp my shoulders. "What's wrong? Are you in some kind of trouble? Who does that car belong to?"

I start to open my mouth when my bathroom toilet flushes upstairs.

My stomach drops as my mother's gaze jerks to the stairwell and her mouth turns down in disapproval. *"Ethan Harris.* Get your rear down here so I can lay out the rules of my house while I'm out of town."

I've never heard my mother sound so forceful and protective before. "Mom, that's not Ethan upstairs."

Her focus shifts to me, perplexed. "I know that's not Lainey's car. So whose is it, Inara?"

"It's mine," my dad says in a low tone as he comes down the stairs, his jacket slung over his arm and his hat in his hand. Stepping off the last stair, he nods to acknowledge my mom. "Hello, Elizabeth."

The look of hurt and betrayal on my mom's suddenly pale face as her hands fall from my shoulders jabs me hard in the gut. "Why is he here, Inara?"

My dad steps forward. "Why don't you let me explain—?"

"Don't!" my mom snaps, holding her hand up. Pink flushes her cheeks. She looks at me and speaks slowly, her tone rigid and full of conviction. "I'm going to go upstairs now, and when I come back down I want the kitchen spotless and this living room cleaned up. Got it?"

I gulp back my shock and nod mutely. She's pretending like he's not even here. That's not a good sign.

Satisfied with my response, she marches past my dad, hangs her coat on the rack, then grabs her overnight bag and walks upstairs, her back ramrod straight.

I wince when her bedroom door shuts firmly, then offer my dad an apologetic grimace. "That um, didn't go so well."

But he's not looking at me. He's staring up the stairwell, a half smile on his face. "God, I miss watching her get feisty like that."

Shaking my head, I tug on his arm to pull him out of whatever memory he's reliving. "You need to go. As in right now. I have never seen Mom this livid."

After setting his hat on his head, my dad shrugs into his jacket. I do the same, following him outside to his car.

Dad opens his car door, but instead of getting in right away he stares back at the house, a contemplative look on his face. "I didn't think it was possible to fall more in love with your mom, but just seeing her in person after so long brings it all back."

My stomach churns at his obliviousness to the way Mom just acted. That wasn't normal for her at all. He can't just show up unannounced. He needs to know…

"Dad?"

"Hmmm?" he glances down at me.

"Mom's seeing someone now. His name's David."

My father's brow furrows and a trace of uncertainty reflects in his eyes. "This must be fairly recent."

I nod.

"Is it serious?"

I shrug. "He makes her happy. Happier than she's been in a long time." Then again, maybe my father does need to know a bit about our past, so he'll tread a little more lightly with Mom. "Your leaving really hurt her. Bad."

Sadness and regret creeps into his expression. "You know I never meant to hurt her."

I nod. "You hurt me too. A lot, but once I saw the videos, I could understand that constant tug of 'interfere or not' you had to deal with. The videos helped me see your perspective. I've experienced that same feeling ever since my dreams started. Give me a chance to show Mom the videos by myself. Then we'll go from there."

"I'd really like to talk to her, but I can see she's not ready."

"I think the videos will help. But I'll talk to her and tell her about me and how you and I first reconnected."

"Sounds like a good way to ease her into the discussion." His expression softens and he touches my chin with his knuckle. "You sound so grown up. It's a bit hard to reconcile my last memory of the little girl who liked me to read her bedtime stories with the young woman you are today."

"Well, I *am* all grown up now, Dad." Smiling, I tuck my hands in my jacket pockets. "Where are you staying?"

He pulls his hat off his head and tosses it in the seat. "With Sage. She insisted. Said we had a lot of lost time to make up for."

"I get that." I'm a bit jealous his sister will get to spend so much time with him.

My dad grins. "Don't worry. You couldn't pry me out of your life now…Fate be damned."

As I start to back away, my dad says, "About Ethan…"

I pause and frown, not liking the harsher edge in his tone. "What about him?"

He shakes his head, his mouth tensing. "I don't want you seeing him."

How can he not like Ethan? I'm sure if he got to know him he'd like him, but the stubborn set of my father's jaw doesn't bode well for him being open to that suggestion. "Are you kidding me? You wouldn't even be here if it weren't for him. He gave you your life back."

His shoulders tense and he grips the car's doorframe tight. "And I'm not going to waste any of it worrying about you. I might not be able to see your future any more, but I'm

14

not going to sit back and say nothing about the danger in your present. And this boy is danger personified. He's on-the-edge. He yanked you into his dream world when I specifically told him not to—"

"But, Dad…" *his Corvus did that, not Ethan.* "I told you I fell asleep. Ethan couldn't control that." My dad doesn't know anything about the Corvus side of things. He only knows Fate is real; he doesn't know demons, angels and Corvus exist too, and Ethan doesn't want me to tell him. Ugh!

My dad's already shaking his head. "Ethan killed that awful creature in his dream with perfectly executed skills, like a professional, Nari. All of it felt incredibly real, not just the part with Fate. How can anyone have a horrible dream like that and not wake up freaked out? Yet he was perfectly calm. I got the impression that he's more familiar with those kind of dreams than you think. He's going to lead you down the wrong path. I feel it in my gut."

Oh, Dad, you have no clue. According to Michael, I'm the one who's supposed to do the path-leading to ensure he takes the right one. I can't believe what I'm hearing from my father. "Ethan's one of the strongest people I know. Stop judging. You've been in my life all of five minutes. You don't really know me, and you don't know him, so you don't get to say who is or isn't right for me."

Frustration flashes across my father's face, then his mouth sets in a stubborn line. "If his dreams are always like that one I witnessed, you most definitely don't need him in your life. Nothing good can come from it."

My heart jerks to my throat. I hope my dad doesn't talk to his sister about Ethan. If he does, Aunt Sage will tell him that Ethan does have constant nightmares, which will only support my father's negative views about my boyfriend. Frustration bolsters my resolve and I tilt my chin up.

"Ethan is a good person and I'm done discussing him with you."

I turn to walk away and my dad says, "I gave up my own happiness for over a decade to keep you safe. You might not think I've been in your life, but you never left my thoughts. Every single day. I'm your father and will always want to protect you. And Nari?"

The expectant terseness in his tone demands that I respond. Folding my arms, I turn back to him slowly. "What?"

His green eyes hold mine, full of parental judgment. "Empty your trash before your mother sees it."

"Huh?"

I frown in confusion and pull my phone from my pocket as he drives away.

Aunt Sage picks up on the second ring. "Hi, Inara. How'd your visit with your dad go, sweetie?"

I stroll up my driveway and sigh heavily. "Actually that's what I'm calling you about."

"Uh oh, you don't sound too happy. What's wrong?"

"It's just...I pause and shove my free hand in my jean pocket. "Dad has decided he really doesn't like Ethan, all because of his dreams. I think that's totally unfair. Ethan gave him his life back. That should give him major props."

My aunt sighs. "You have to look at this from your dad's perspective. He just wants what's best for you."

"Ethan *is* what's best for me. He makes me happy, Aunt Sage. I know Dad is going to ask you if Ethan has nightmares all the time. Please don't tell him that he does."

"I won't lie to him, Inara. If he asks, I have to tell him the truth, but I'll also tell him how you two are together. I know Ethan cares very much for you. I think that'll help."

"It can't hurt," I grumble.

"Speaking of Ethan's dreams, I've been studying up on

different techniques to try to help him learn to expel that awful imagery from his mind while he sleeps. I'd be happy to work with him."

Since she doesn't know the truth behind the source of Ethan's nightmares, I don't know if she can really help. I hedge my answer. "I'll see what he says."

"Wonderful. I'm ready and willing if he'll let me."

I head toward my front porch. But what if my aunt really could help Ethan get control of his dreams? Then my father wouldn't have anything to hold over him. Hope lifts the weight on my chest. "Thanks, Aunt Sage. I'll definitely ask him about it."

Hanging up, I start to reach for my front door, and the reason my dad made that parting comment about emptying my trash hits me. Wrappers. My face instantly flames with embarrassed heat. Ugh, the trashcan is right beside the toilet. My dad knows Ethan and I had sex last night. Now I know why he's being so incredibly negative about Ethan.

I've seen the way Lainey's dad has acted over my best friend's safety in the past, and her boyfriend, Matt, has joked about how her father has reminded him, more than once, that he's a crack shot at the police station's firing range. Apparently, fathers maintain a level of parental protectiveness over their daughters that could rival a Presidential security detail.

Any hopes I had for getting Dad to like Ethan are pretty much in the trash right along with those wrappers. Sighing my frustration, I walk inside.

CHAPTER 2

NARA

"*H*ey!" Ethan looks surprised as he opens his door. "I thought you'd be spending the rest of the day with your dad."

I sigh heavily, then reach for his hand and walk inside. When I continue to tug him with me, he asks, "What's wrong?" But I don't say anything. I let him shut the door before I pull him into the living room.

Ethan's hand tightens on mine while I lead him to the couch. When I slide onto his lap and tuck my head on his shoulder instead of sitting beside him like I normally would, he instantly spears his fingers in my hair, his hand flexing against the back of my scalp. "Nara, you're worrying me. What happened with your dad?"

If seeing Ethan's Christmas tree twinkling with white lights and stringed popcorn in the corner of the living room doesn't bring a smile to my face—the idea of two guys sitting around stringing popcorn and cranberries is beyond hilarious and adorable at the same time—I know I'm in a sad place. I tuck my nose under his jaw and breathe in his calming smell, relishing the feel of his strong arms holding me close. "I just want to sit like this for a little bit if that's okay."

His tense hold loosens, and his fingers slide through my hair. He exhales, then kisses me on the forehead. "Okay. I'll wait until you're ready to talk."

I close my eyes while Ethan adjusts us to be more comfortable. He's so warm I can't help but snuggle closer and sigh in contentment. Here, with him, I don't have to think about my dad or mom. Leaning against his solid chest, it hurts a little less when I mentally replay the look in my mother's eyes once she finally came out of her room and blew past me, mumbling, "I have some last minute shopping to do. I'll be back later."

"But, Mom. I want to talk to you."

"Not now, Inara. I just..." Pausing, she brushed her bangs out of her eyes and straightened her shoulders. "Not right now." And then, she left.

I listen to Ethan's even breathing and the sound of his heart beat thumping at a slow, calm pace. He's my rock. The one person I know I can depend on. Inhaling his clean, masculine scent, I finally lift my head and grimace. "So yeah, things pretty much went south when my mom arrived early."

Ethan's dark eyebrows shoot high. "She came home while your dad was still there?"

I lace my fingers with the hand he'd rested on my thigh. "Yeah. Of course, I haven't shown my mom the videos yet, because I'd planned to do that within a day of my dad coming, sometime *after* Christmas. Instead, all my mom sees is her daughter sneaking around behind her back and hanging out with the man who abandoned them both without explanation over a decade ago."

Ethan slowly runs his thumb over mine. "So what happened?"

Once I relay everything from this morning—well, minus my dad's comments about our relationship. It's not like I'm going to stop seeing Ethan—he shakes his head. "I'm sorry, Nara. Maybe once your mom gets back from her errands, she'll have calmed down enough to talk to you. I'm sure discovering your dad there wasn't easy for her."

I nod quickly. "I totally understand her anger and sense of betrayal. What bothers me is the fact that she couldn't look me in the eye. That really hurt. I can't imagine my mom not looking at me ever again when she talks to me."

Clasping my cheek, he turns my eyes to his. "Samson didn't look at me directly for several days after I woke up in the hospital. I think it's a defense mechanism."

I swallow, hope filling my heart. He'd been through the same thing. "Defense mechanism?"

Ethan slides his thumb along my jawline, a brief look of sadness in his eyes. "Remember how you refused to look at me when I first woke up in the hospital? I tried, but you wouldn't meet my gaze." When I sniff and nod, he offers a half-smile. "Of course, I flipped when you left my room, but now I know only someone who still cares about you will react like this. They feel betrayed and need to work through it in their head first. Otherwise, they wouldn't bother. That's why you left, right?"

When I nod, he says, "Give your mom her space. She'll come to you wanting answers, like you did me."

I laugh at that, the weight on my heart lifting a little. I wrap my arms around his neck. "Or demanding them, huh?"

He grunts, then smiles and folds his arms around my waist, pulling me close. "Exactly."

"Thanks for talking me down. My dad seemed to admire Mom getting all feisty, but I've never seen her 'silent-treatment' angry before. It freaked me out. I just wish there was something I could do. I hate feeling so helpless. Like I should've said something before now."

Ethan shakes his head and presses a kiss to my temple. "You can't make it right for everyone, Sunshine. Your parents have to decide on their own. This is the time of year when families usually ban together. I'm sure that's making you extra sad, especially with your dad back in your life, but no amount of..."

When Ethan trails off, I sit up. He's staring into space as if he were contemplating something. "What are you thinking about?"

He looks at me and lifts an eyebrow. "The holidays gave me an idea. I'm not sure if it might help, but I don't see how it can hurt."

I rest my hands on his shoulders. "Go on."

"It'll require some scouting." Grinning, he grips my hips, then glances toward the window. "Out in the cold and definitely traipsing through a bit of snow. Think you're up for it?"

I quickly slide off his lap and stand, waving for him to follow. "What do you have in mind?"

"Mistletoe," he says as he stands and stretches.

"Mistletoe?"

He nods and immediately lowers his arms to hook them around my waist, pulling me close. "It's appropriate for Christmas, but it's also a tradition; not only does it provide protection and peace while it's hung in doorways, but no one can pass under it without kissing someone."

"Mistletoe," I pause and gesture to his Christmas tree, "Popcorn and cranberries...I had no idea you were so traditional."

Ethan glances at the tree in the corner, a pained half-smile on his lips. "I have many needle holes in my thumbs to prove otherwise. There is definitely stuff you still don't know about me."

Smiling, I nod. "I have to admit, I didn't expect the garland. I love it, by the way."

He laughs. "All Samson's bright idea. Maybe having our parents in the same town inspired him to want to relive a happier time in our childhood or something. It had sounded like a great plan when he suggested it, but the reality of just how much length you need to decorate a whole tree had us cursing each other in no time." He sighs and shrugs. "It's done now at least. Next year we're buying fake garland like normal people do."

"No, you're not! Don't you dare skip such a neat Christmas tradition. I'll help next year, and I'll even bring some holiday spiced cider to enjoy while we're working on it."

The blue in Ethan's eyes deepens and his hold on me tightens. "It's a date."

I eye him with amused suspicion and rest my hands on his chest. "Now about this mistletoe. How do I know this isn't just another excuse to kiss me?"

He drops a quick kiss on my lips. "I'll never pass up an opportunity to kiss you; however, mistletoe *is* special. Its mystical qualities can be especially potent if you harvest it from the highest branch of a white oak hundreds of years old. The older the tree, the stronger the mistletoe's power."

I curl my fingers against his soft thermal shirt. "That sounds very specific. How do you know this?"

Bafflement crosses his face, and he slowly shakes his head. "I have no idea."

Tapping his chest, I smile. "Must be your Corvus sharing some of his eons-old knowledge. I take it you at least know where we can find a hundreds-year old oak with mistletoe growing on it?"

A cocky grin rides his face. "Yep, but we'd better get going. It snowed more in the northern areas of Virginia this morning, so the snow will be deeper there, making it harder to get to. I have to be back here to pick Samson up at the airport at two. His car's in the shop right now. And I'll need to stop by a sports store first, then we can swing by your house and pick up snow boots. Sound good?"

"Sports store?" I ask, tilting my head.

Ethan laughs. "You'll see."

I smile and push up on my toes to wrap my arms around his neck. Kissing his jaw, I whisper, "Thank you. A day of adventure with you sounds perfect."

ETHAN

I LOOK over at Nara biting her bottom lip. She's worrying over her mom and David getting closer while her dad's now back in her life. Grasping the steering wheel, I give up trying to get her to guess what's in the sports store bag, and clasp her hand, offering my warmth. She doesn't even notice, she's so deep in thought. All I want to do is make it right for her. She always sees the good in others. Even now, I know she hopes her parents will work things out. And for her sake I hope they do.

Unlike my screwed up family, hers might actually have a chance now that my Corvus laid the smack down on Fate. I actually owe him for that. Scaring the hell out of Fate was the best thing the raven spirit could've done for her. At least now, that spiteful amorphous entity will leave Nara and her family in peace.

When she sat there in my arms on the couch earlier, so still and silent, my heart dropped. I've never felt so helpless.

Nara is always so positive, and to see her so upset stripped me bare. I didn't know what to say to make her feel better. That's why I was surprised when the idea for the mistletoe came to me. I knew the knowledge wasn't mine, but the intent, the desire to make her smile again…hell yeah, that was all me.

I pull through the woods and park my car. When I skim over the sunlight reflecting off her blonde hair and vivid green eyes, my heart actually aches. I love her that much. Last night was freaking amazing. I didn't want to leave her this morning. All I wanted to do was clasp her hand and pull her back into bed so I could spend the day loving her from head to toe. I wanted to bask in her sweet smell and run my fingers along her soft skin all over again. For as long as she'd let me.

Last night wasn't just sex. It was an epiphany, not just that I was right about us being perfect together physically, but it proved what I knew in my heart—that I'd never feel complete without her. The peace that I felt while she slept in my arms left me shaking. I watched her sleep until my eyes couldn't stay open any longer. I just didn't want our night to end. It's like I knew that as soon as my eyes closed, we'd be yanked away from each other, from *us*, once more.

I shut off the engine, my love for Nara punching me in the gut as I turn to look at her. That another person can hold so much sway over my inner calm should scare the absolute shit out of me. I've worked so hard to control my reactions to all the negative and evil stimuli around me. Yet from the day Nara crossed my path, she crashed through my controlled façade with her own special brand of amazing. And she's never stopped looking forward since; she never lost hope. Not for me. Not for anyone.

Until today.

Above all else, I will always want to keep her safe, but

second to that, I'll do everything in my power to make her happy.

When she smiles, sunshine rains down on me, and all I want to do is soak in its warm, cleansing rays. The darkness only lives in the corners when Nara's by my side.

Today, I'm going to give my Sunshine her hope back.

NARA

Ethan has spent the last fifteen minutes trying to distract me from my thoughts. After I'd stopped by my house for snow boots, he picked up something from the sports store. But even though he keeps trying to get me to guess what's inside the red plastic bag sitting on the car seat between us, it isn't enough to pull me out of my conflicted musings. All I can think about is the Christmas store explosion that had gone off in my living room while I'd been at his house.

When I walked in the door to get my snow boots, Mom and David were putting up a brand new Christmas tree. The fake tree was massive and sported thick branches that made it look incredibly real and near picture perfect. Boxes of new ornaments, garland, and additional lights littered every bit of furniture, waiting to be put on the tree. The whole lot must've cost her a fortune.

I tried to quietly bypass them, but when Mom saw me start to head upstairs, she smiled and told me to come help them decorate the new tree together. Relieved I had other plans, I said, "Sorry, Mom. Ethan and I are heading out to do some… last minute shopping" —*for mistletoe and all the wishes it'll entail.*

While David wished me luck on my shopping, none of Mom's earlier anger showed on her face. Instead, she just nodded her understanding to my excuse, then started to hum to the Christmas song playing in the background as she moved around the Christmas tree, May-pole-style, with a string of multicolored lights of purple, red, teal and blue. Yeah, I couldn't get back out to Ethan's car fast enough.

Lifting my hand from my lap, Ethan kisses my knuckles, drawing my focus. "It'll all work out, Nara. You have to believe that."

I blink at the snow-covered clearing in front of us, the pond to our left, and the stand of trees surrounding us. "We're here already? I must've really zoned."

Ethan slides his thumb over my knuckles, and understanding reflects in his blue eyes "I left you to your thoughts, but now we're here to cheer you up."

Right then, the noon sun slowly slides out from behind the gray clouds. When its bright rays spill across the secluded space, the blanket of undisturbed snow surrounding the pond begins to sparkle, as if someone has scattered a layer of diamond dust across it.

"It's gorgeous!" A smile spreads on my face, and my fingers tighten around Ethan's. "If that's not a good sign, I don't know what is."

"I couldn't agree more."

My attention slides back to Ethan, but he's not looking at the snow; he's staring at me.

I squeeze our clasped hands. "Thank you for bringing me here. Even if we don't find the mistletoe, seeing this reminds me that things might seem dull and gray, but brightness always finds a way to burst through."

Ethan smiles and shakes his head. "Oh, ye of little faith. We'll definitely find some mistletoe. Get your boots on."

While I pull off my thick socks and tug on my fur-lined boots, I frown at his jeans covering his black combat boots. "Those won't protect your feet, Ethan. The snow out there has to be at least six inches deep."

He just laughs, then opens his car door. "Come on slow poke. We have some mistletoe to gather."

A few minutes later, wishing I could've found my gray scarf, I finish zipping up my coat and meet him by the edge of the pond. My breath gusts out in swirls of frost while I eye his thin army jacket over a thermal shirt and jeans. "Where's your winter jacket? It's thirty degrees. You're going to freeze to death out here."

Ethan shifts his attention from the massive tree close to the pond back to me. "Actually, it's twenty-four-point-seven."

I blink at him. "Um, that was pretty exact. Are you a human thermometer now too?"

"Apparently." He shakes his head, a bemused smile tugging at his lips. "I just *know* the temperature."

Stomping the snow off my boots, I snicker. "From now on I'm texting you for the daily weather report so I'll know how to dress. Seriously though, aren't you cold?"

In answer, Ethan tucks his hand under my hair, cupping the back of my neck.

His toasty touch sends a zing of warmth all the way to my toes. I give a wry smile. "That's just not fair."

He smiles and slides his thumb along my neck. "Consider me your own personal body heater."

I snort. "You do that *without* touching me."

Chuckling, Ethan releases me to point to the branches that spread out from the massive tree he'd been looking at. "I remembered this oak from our visit here before. Do you see the mistletoe up there?"

The round bunches of green are the only color decorating the tree's bare branches. I squint past the sunlight filtering through. "Yeah, I see it, but that has to be at least three stories high. How are we going to get to it?"

Ethan eyes the mistletoe and rocks on his heels. "Well, some people shoot it down."

"Shoot it?" I swing my attention back to him, eyes wide. "You didn't buy a gun from that sports store, did you? The bag didn't look big enough for that."

He scowls slightly. "I don't like guns. Plus, gunshots would draw attention that we're on private property—this time without an invitation. Are you ready to guess what's in the bag now?"

"I don't have a clue."

Ethan shakes his head as he steps back over to his car. "You'd make a terrible game show contestant."

"A BB gun?"

He shuts his car door with the red bag in hand and a contemplative look on his face. "I didn't think of a BB gun. That would've worked, I suppose. Though this is more fun."

Snow kicks up around his boots and sticks to the bottom of his jeans once he makes his way back over to my side.

"So what is it?" I ask, impatient.

Ethan pulls the handle out of the bag, a wide grin spreading across his face. "A slingshot."

"That's your weapon of choice? Hmmm, I think my BB gun suggestion would've been better."

"What? You don't think I have what it takes?"

I gesture to the slingshot while he squats to push snow out of his way. "Those are highly inaccurate and not as powerful as a BB gun, especially one with a CO_2 cartridge giving it some extra power."

He eyes me from his squatted position. "How do you know so much about BB guns?"

"'Cause I own one. If you'd have told me how you planned to get the mistletoe down, I could've brought mine."

His dark brows pull together. "What do you shoot with your BB gun?"

"Cans, Ethan. Just cans. Later when I got better, it was leaves, tree branches and stuff. Learning to shoot—versus being shot upon as a goalie—with any kind of accuracy is a skill I had to develop, not one that came from dreaming it the night before." I pause. "Speaking of shooting, I haven't done it in a long time. That might be kind of fun to do together some time."

"How about we start with this for now," Ethan says. Standing, he puts a small, cold stone in my hand, then holds out the slingshot.

"You want me to try?"

"Why not?"

I start to hand him back the stone. "I've never done it before."

"Then I'll show you." He flashes a confident smile and moves behind me. Setting the slingshot in my other hand, he shows me how to set the stone inside the leather and pinch it closed around it. Then, he lifts my arms and directs me how to pull the slingshot back. While I ready my aim, he rests his hands on my hips and leans close to whisper in my ear, "I want many of your firsts to be with me, Sunshine."

His firm grip tightening on my hips and his husky voice radiating in my ear send the rock flying before I'm ready. I snort when it makes a spectacular arc right straight down into the pond. "David would *so* not want me on his team against Goliath."

Ethan chuckles. "You're not aiming for a monstrous giant's head. Just some mistletoe."

"Like that's so much easier."

He sets another stone in my hand. "Try again."

After three more attempts, I at least got the rock as high

as the mistletoe, but it lost steam and quickly fell before getting anywhere near the greenery.

Sighing, I hand him the slingshot. "Your turn. Hopefully your aim is far better than mine."

After retrieving some more rocks, Ethan sets one in the slingshot, then closes one eye as he pulls the rock back. "For the mystical power of the mistletoe," he says, then releases the leather.

The rock shoots out of the slingshot so fast and hard, I can't track it, but a couple seconds later, I see a bundle of mistletoe the size of a soccer ball tilt sideways in the tree.

"Dead on!" I say and clap in appreciation. "One more hit should bring it down."

Ethan sends another rock flying. Two seconds later, the greenery tumbles down...landing in the middle of the pond.

Pouting, I scan the massive oak for other options. "Crud. The only bundles are in the branches reaching out over the water. Any other mistletoe you break free will end up in the same place." As if mocking me, the floating mistletoe hits some ice, then ever-so-slowly sinks under the water. I glance his way and sigh. "Now what are we going to do?"

CHAPTER 3

NARA

*E*than stands by the pond, shirtless and in the process of stepping out of his boots and socks.

"You are *not* going in that water."

He touches my chin, a slight smile tilting his lips. "Do you know your cheeks get rosy when you're all worked up?"

I slice my hand toward the huge pieces of ice floating in the pond's surface. "Your brain will shut down. The water's too cold."

Ethan's brow furrows. "We just talked about this. I'm not cold. At all. I'll be fine."

His fingers might feel warm on my skin, but I jerk my head back and forth. "It's one thing to be able to withstand cooler outside temperatures, but you don't know how your body will react in freezing water."

"You've studied ravens, Nara. How do you think they survive, even in arctic environments?"

I shuffle through my memory, seeking an answer even as I mumble, "They certainly don't go swimming in freezing ponds." By the time I glance up, Ethan has already stepped barefoot in the snow to the pond's edge.

"Ethan, no!"

He just grins at me and walks into the water. My heart jerks when he shallow dives, disappearing under the water's surface. Remembering he'd told me that he always keeps a change of clothes in his car in case a demon hunt turns messy, I tromp through the snow and open his car door. Once I pop the trunk, I hurry to the back to pull out a water-proof duffle bag.

I lug the bag over to the pond's edge and set it down to glance at my watch, my heart racing with worry. Ethan's been under for three minutes. How long can he hold his breath, and how long does it take for hypothermia to set in?

Another minute passes and my bottom lip is pretty much gnawed to bits. My chest aches and my eyes sting as I stare with fierce intensity at the now smooth-as-glass pond top where he dove in, willing him back to the surface.

Nothing.

"Ethan." My voice sounds hoarse and strained and I start to hyperventilate, my breathing coming in fast, frantic bursts. A rush of arctic wind whips around me, and when the fog from my breath morphs into the words, TELL HIM, I grit my teeth and snap, "I work on my time frame, not yours, Fate." The fact more time has passed without sight of Ethan sends me off the deep end. "Go before I tell him you're back to bullying me again. Or this time around, I might not stop him from shredding you."

The second the words hanging in the air dissipate, I open my mouth to scream Ethan's name, but the smooth water starts to ripple, making me pause. When Ethan's dark head breaks the surface, tears streak down my cheeks.

I quickly brush them away and bend to unzip his bag. Grabbing the towel sitting on top of the clothes, I straighten to see Ethan climbing up the embankment, his raven wings growing larger with each step he takes.

"Nara." He stands next to me, dripping frigid water into the snow under his feet.

I'm so upset, I refuse to look at him or his gorgeous wings while I rub the towel in brisk strokes across his hard chest. "That has to be the most reckless, stupidest thing you've ever done."

"Nara," he repeats in a calming tone, but I don't want to hear any excuses. I just want him dry and warm. I run the towel over his shoulders, then along the side of his neck.

Ethan tosses the mistletoe into the snow beside his bag, then captures my wrists to stop my frantic movements. "Look at me."

His voice is firm, commanding. The fact that his hands aren't blocks of ice eases some of my panic. I shift my attention to his blue one.

"Come with me," he says, taking a step back toward the water.

My eyes widen in panic. "I can't go in there. I *will* turn into a human popsicle."

"Trust me, Sunshine." At the same time Ethan grips my hand, his raven wings unfurl fully behind him in an impressive, breathtaking spread.

I stare wide-eyed at their strength and beauty. When he'd shown them to me before, we'd been in my small bedroom, so he hadn't been able to spread them as wide. The sun reflects off the streaks of iridescent purples, blues, and greens veining along the midnight black feathers, only adding to their mystical appearance.

Tugging the towel from my tight hold, Ethan releases me to quickly dry his hair, chest, and arms. I can't help but watch his muscles and abs flex with his quick movements. Once he drops the towel on his bag, he reaches for the zipper on my jacket. My heart speeds up as he slides it down. When the zipper pulls free of the hook, I finally manage to breathe out, "I can't, Ethan. I won't survive that."

"You can," he simply states, stepping close to tug my coat off. When my coat joins the towel on top of his bag, he laces his fingers with mine, the desire swirling in his deep blue eyes pulling me in. "I want to share this with you, Nara. Please let me."

Even though I'm shivering against the cold, the look of assured certainty on his face warms me from the inside out. I bite my lip and start to slide off my left boot. Once my foot's free, Ethan's hands encircle my waist and he effortlessly lifts me toward him.

The moment my legs settle around his waist, I kick off the other boot, then gasp at the jarring cold of his wet jeans seeping into mine. Darkness suddenly surrounds my back and lifts my thighs. A second later I'm settled against him once more—minus the cold dampness.

His wings move closer, folding fully around my back and encircling my legs and feet in a layer of soft warmth.

I glance up at the blue sky and see puffs of clouds above us where his wings haven't completely closed yet. Matching Ethan's confident smile, I wrap my arms around his neck. "Show me something new." I lean close to kiss his jaw, but Ethan turns his head and presses his lips to mine instead. I sigh against his mouth as his fingers massage my skin before his arms gather me even closer and the silky darkness encloses around us.

I feel us moving, but I'm distracted by Ethan's heady kiss and lost in his masculine, earthy smell. This kind of magical connection is like a double whammy to my senses, heightening the experience of loving him.

The bubbly, muffled sound of water moving all around me feels strange. Goose bumps raise on my arms, and I break our kiss for a second to reach out and push against his wing. The slight gurgle of the water's movement and buoying pressure moving away then rushing back against his wing and my palm makes me gasp.

"Amazing," I whisper in awe. I sense the sharp bite of the cold water around us; its sterile smell is in the air, but I don't feel its chilling effect. Ethan kisses the line of my jaw, sensuously making his way back to my mouth, building fiery warmth inside me.

Excitement overrides my apprehension, and I let Ethan's lips claim mine; all I feel is the strength of his arms around me, the mesmerizing drug of his kisses devastating my senses, and the erotic sensation of his strong wings cocooning inward, sliding along my butt and thighs, cupping me tighter against him. The combination is intoxicating. I moan against his mouth and tighten my grip on his neck, trying to get closer.

Silky, strong feathers begin to slide and tuck themselves even tighter along my calves. Caressing the muscles, they wind their way down to the bottom of my bare feet. I whimper my delight and curl my toes to capture some of the soft vanes, holding them captive. Ethan's grip on me constricts and his groan of desire rumbles through his chest before he deepens our kiss, his tongue entangling with mine, amping our intimacy.

I lose all sense of place and time during our underwater heavy kissing session, but when it starts getting harder to breathe, Ethan breaks our passionate kiss. Once we start to move again, he presses less intense kisses to my chin, my lips, my nose, my cheekbones and then to my forehead, worshiping every part of my face.

As daylight slowly splinters through and breathing becomes easier, I tuck my face in the warm, secure place between his shoulder and his jaw and quietly blink back my tears of amazement. "Thank you for not letting me be too chicken to dive in; that was an indescribably beautiful experience. One I'll never forget."

He clasps my waist in a firm grip, and as his wings start to separate above us, he presses his jaw against mine, locking me to him, his voice raw with emotion. "Thank you for trusting me enough to try. You have no idea how much that means to me."

When I lift my head, he brushes a lone tear off my cheek with his thumb, a smug look on his face. "Moved you, huh?"

I nod, then give him an impish smile. "You know you're going to have to do that again, don't you?"

"I think I've created a monster," he says on a laugh, stepping up onto the embankment. His jeans are dripping once more, but every other part of him is bone dry, just like me. While he effortlessly holds me above the snow while I slide my feet into my boots, I'm even more in awe of his strength. We've been in enough dangerous situations in the past— adrenaline pumping, tension running high—that it would've been so easy for him to hurt me by accident, but he never has.

Feet firmly planted on the ground, I shrug into my coat, then throw him the towel so he can sop up the wetness from his jeans.

After he's mostly dry, I bend to retrieve the mistletoe while he grabs his bag and heads over to open his back door, sliding into his backseat to change into dry clothes.

I make my way to his open back door, my heart racing a little while I inspect the bundle of greenery sporting red berries. "Ethan?"

"Yeah?"

"Do we need the berries for the mistletoe to be effective? I'm worried about Houdini. Most things like this are poisonous to pets."

He leans toward the opening, his dark eyebrows raised. "You expect him to jump all the way to the top of the doorway to get to it?"

I snort. "No, but as it dries out, the berries could loosen and fall. That's my worry."

"Break off a small piece and pluck out the berries."

I snap off a twig, then set the bigger bundle on top of his car next to his damp towel. "Now what?" I say, holding the sprig on the roof while I bend down to see his face.

Ethan quickly leans over and kisses me, then glances to the roof, grinning up at the bit of mistletoe he knows I'm inadvertently holding over his head. "Nope, still works."

I roll my eyes, but smile. Shrugging out of my jacket, I toss it in the front seat so the bulk won't hinder me while I lean on the car's roof to pull out every single berry I can find. I'm almost done, when Ethan says, "Hey, can you hand me that towel?"

Swiping the berries off his roof into the snow, I absently lower the towel for him to grab, while I examine the bundle of greenery for any berries I might've missed.

"Thanks." He tugs and the towel disappears from my fingers. I brace myself against the cold air biting at my bare cheeks and fingers and spin the mistletoe around in my palms one last time. When the cool air blows up my shirt, I release the shiver I'd been holding back. A couple seconds later a sudden warmth flows along my belly quickly chasing the chill away. I slow my movements, then pause at the sensation of the warmth moving down my belly button to the top of my jeans. "Ethan?"

"Come here. I want to show you something."

As soon as I bend down to see what he wants, he clasps my wrist and pulls me across his lap.

Giggling, I quickly flip over onto my back and try to sit up, but he presses his hand to my stomach. Spreading his fingers wide to hold me in place, he slides my boots off into the snow outside the car. "One of these days I'll get to wake up with you in my arms." His husky tone glides across my skin like a tender caress as his deep blue gaze skims along my jean-clad legs.

Clasping my ankle, he lifts my bare foot up and traces his thumb down the center from my toes to my heel. "But for now…there's no water, no wings. Just you, and me, and a very cozy backseat." He turns my foot and my pulse skips as he presses a tender kiss just under my toes, then another on the ball of my foot, and yet another, longer lingering kiss along my arch before raising a dark eyebrow. "Care to take it for a spin?"

He's wearing dry jeans, but hasn't put his shirt on yet, and the sight of his gorgeous body and feel of his muscular thighs underneath me, coupled with his sensual suggestion, melts my insides. I lift his hand from my belly and press light kisses from the top of his palm to the bottom, then finish with a slow answering kiss on the TTTWFO tattoo along his wrist.

Before I can say a word, Ethan's fingers curl around the back of my neck. One second I'm on my back and the next I'm upright in his lap.

I don't remember moving—his reflexes are that quick—but Ethan's mouth pressing against mine in a deep, soul-searching kiss, sets off a flurry of electrical surges flowing through me so fast and furious I'm left breathless by their fierce intensity.

Just as I move my hand to his jaw, something makes a loud squawk, drawing our attention.

Patch is standing just outside the open door on the toe of my boot. Tilting his head back, he swallows a red berry, then he spreads his wings slightly and begins to sway back and forth. All the berries I plucked from the mistletoe are gone.

"What?" I ask the bird, laughing. A raven eating the berries doesn't worry me; they can eat just about anything.

He bobs his head up and down, making several *gronking* sounds. I shake my head. "It's not my fault you gobbled them down so quickly. There might be some more under my boot." I snicker. "But you'll have to move it to find out."

When the raven lets out a loud *raaaaack*, Ethan looks at me, his brows pulled together. "You actually understand him?"

I nod, a bit surprised. "Yeah, I do. I get the gist of what he wants. He's very direct." I gesture to the bird. "Don't you?"

Ethan slowly shakes his head. "Every other animal I understand, but it's like Patch is a blank slate. I might be able to get him to understand me when I really concentrate, but I don't hear or sense exactly what he wants like I do other animals."

Patch had been plucking at the boot's shoestring while we spoke, but so far it wasn't moving. Turning to us, he flaps his wings hard and squawks long and loud.

"Go to the top of the oak and gorge yourself." Ethan grunts, then slams the door shut, cutting off Patch's sounds of agitation.

I laugh and pat his jaw. "Did you actually understand him that time?"

His hands flex on my hips, his thumbs sliding under my shirt to trail along my skin just above my jeans. "Not a bit, but he's taking up what little time we have together."

My brow furrows. "I'm kind of surprised you can't understand him."

"You're the only one I care about connecting with, Sunshine," Ethan says between kisses as he shifts my thigh over his until I'm straddling his lap.

His double meaning makes me tingle all over. I settle

against him and smile. "You *were* in the process of showing me the benefits of backseat love over Corvus submarining."

"Submarining, huh?" Chuckling, Ethan shifts forward and pulls me flush against his hardness. Before I can reply, he quickly captures my bottom lip between his teeth, but when he starts to slowly slide my lip free, he pulls back and clasps my jaw. "I taste blood." Running his thumb along my lip, he turns it down. "God, Nara. It looks like ground hamburger. Did I do that?"

"No." I shrug and glance away. "I was worried about you while you were underwater."

He palms my cheek. "I'm sorry. I didn't mean to worry you."

I meet his gaze, folding my hand over his. "I know it's the Corvus making you so reckless."

Ethan snorts. "As much as I'd like to lay every dangerous thing I do at the Corvus' feet, I can't, Nara. I've always done things I shouldn't have. My father might've thought I was a saint compared to my stubborn brother..." He shakes his head. "But the difference is, I just didn't flaunt it in his face like Samson did." Cupping my face with both hands, he slides his thumbs along my cheekbones. "But one thing I'll never, ever risk is you. I would never have attempted to take you in that water if I didn't know for sure you'd be safe."

Leaning close, he presses a tender kiss to my lips. "I'll always watch out for you."

"But who's watching out for you?" I reply, loving how his kiss sends sparks shooting through me once more.

He shrugs and unbuttons the top three buttons of my shirt, his mouth crooked in an ironic smile. "I've been responsible for me for a while now."

I shake my head and cup either side of his face like he did mine a second ago. "Not any more, Ethan. I'm watching out for you too. I care what happens to you, so for my sanity

I want you and your Corvus to care about you for *me.* Got it?"

Ethan swallows a couple of times, then blinks away sudden mist in his eyes. "I love you, Nara."

I've never seen him get choked up before. Not like this. He's sharing a deeper layer of himself with me than he ever has before. My smile trembles with emotion. "Sorry, I didn't mean to get all serious on you—"

Ethan kisses me again, but this time he keeps the pressure in check, his kiss tender and searching. "Never stop loving me," he murmurs against my lips.

"No chance of that," I say adamantly while he frees the rest of my buttons, then unsnaps my bra.

As his hands move over my sensitive skin, suddenly clothes are too much constriction and we're fast to rid ourselves of any barrier that keeps us apart, other than protection.

After I settle into his lap, Ethan gently grasps my waist and pulls me fully against him. The feel of his warm, hard chest against my sensitized breasts and his strong arms encircling my back is so thrilling, my cheeks flush with the pure bliss of unrestrained togetherness. He kisses me deeply and intimately, his thumbs tracing sensually along the sides of my breasts. I moan against his mouth and he tugs me closer, upping the tide of passion and desire between us.

Tracing his hands to my lower back, he grasps my hips and lifts me, then tilts my body forward slightly. I mewl softly against his mouth as he lowers me down over him.

"So perfect," he rasps, then whispers loving words against my throat.

This position feels somehow more intimate, and his enticing encouragement gives me both the confidence and freedom to find a rhythm that allows our love to flow naturally. I gasp through the thrilling new sensations zipping through me and grow bolder. Gripping his broad shoulders tight, I let myself go, totally unrestrained.

As we move together, Ethan groans against my mouth. His fingers flex on my hips, then caress my butt before he pulls me tighter to him, his hold desperate and intense. My heart races and my love swells. Tingling heat lingers everywhere his fingers have tracked my skin.

It's like he's leaving a roadmap of every place he's touched. Does he feel it like I do? Am I imagining it? Are these amazing sensations just wishful thinking of a shared connection on my part? All I know is, when we come together like this, it feels stronger, deeper, making each time with Ethan an even more amazing and unique experience.

The inexplicable completeness I feel when we physically connect defies description; the passion that flows between us goes way beyond the physical. If it were possible for two souls to merge, it feels like ours do at the most minute level.

My breath rushes out as Ethan sears my neck with aggressive nips, followed by sweet, tender kisses. He takes me high, then makes me melt until my heart reaches a hummingbird's pace.

Once our breathing begins to slow, his warm hands fold around my back, his hold almost possessive as he kisses the swell of my breasts. When he suddenly slides his tongue between them, lapping up a trickle of sweat, the act is so primal and raw, a shiver of sheer delight ripples through me; all I can do is grip his shoulders with shaky hands and revel in the many emotions he makes me feel.

"My Sunshine," he says, reaching the hollow in my throat. *She wrecks the hell out of me. Every damn time.*

Gasping, I tense. Ethan's eyes snap to mine, worry creasing his brow. "What's wrong? Did you hate that? I'm sorry, I couldn't resist. You just taste so good."

I blink back tears and smile past my surprise. Did I really

just hear his thoughts? When I don't hear anything else, I shake my head. Must be my overactive imagination. "No, I didn't hate it at all. You just surprised me."

A sinful smile tilts his lips. "Did you like that surprise?"

I wrap my arms around his neck and lay my head on his shoulder. "If it's with you, like this…I'll never get tired of surprises." Pressing a kiss to his neck, I inhale and enjoy his outdoorsy smell mixed with his masculine deodorant.

Ethan chuckles and wraps his arms around my waist. "Good, 'cause I'm always going to want to make you my own personal lollypop."

His comment makes my insides quiver. Smiling, I run my tongue along his collarbone, saying, "Mmm, you taste really good right here. I wonder if you taste different in other places…"

Ethan groans and lifts me upright, his eyes blazing with heat. "Are you trying to drive me crazy?"

I frown. "Why would you say that? I thought you'd love the idea of—"

He shakes his head, a frustrated look on his face. "I have to go get Samson soon. Remember?"

I smile and flip my hand. "Well, never mind then."

Strong hands flex on my waist. "Oh no. I'm holding you to that promise."

My eyebrows shoot up. "What promise? I don't remember making any."

Ethan's face reflects determination. "The next time I get you alone, I'm going to tease you non-stop. I'll lick and nibble and kiss you from head to toe…"

I feel my face drain of color. I know firsthand just how good he is at teasing. I shake my head quickly. "No, Ethan."

Pulling me forward, he whispers next to my ear, his voice full of merciless intent. "Be ready to want me *desperately*.

That scar on your palm is going to be working overtime soon, Sunshine."

I involuntarily clamp my hand tight, thinking how easily his touch on my scar sends my hormones into overdrive. Leaning forward, I whisper back, trailing my fingers over his shoulder and down across the top of the sword tattoo gracing his shoulder blade. "You know...ever since you told me this tattoo is sensitive to my touch, it only makes me want to explore it even more."

Ethan hisses in my ear and grips my hand. Lifting it off his shoulder, he laces our fingers together and grunts. "Truce?"

I give him a saucy smile. "For now."

Ethan chuckles the entire time we're getting dressed in the backseat. While I tug on my shirt, he catches my elbow a split second before I ping him in the eye. Then he quickly diverts my foot from hitting a sensitive area as I shrug into my skinny jeans. Settling back into the seat, I offer an apologetic smile. "Sorry. Seemed like a lot more room a few minutes ago."

Shaking his head, he smiles. "It feels good to laugh. I wouldn't trade this experience for anything in the world, Nara." He drops a kiss on my nose. "Moments like this with you are priceless."

I've never seen him so laidback and happy, and I'm glad I had a little something to do with that. Once we're settled in the front seat, he threads his fingers with mine and rests our clasped hands on his thigh, and then we drive out of the woods, heading back to Blue Ridge.

He's so relaxed, I realize now might be a good time to tell him what Michael said. That maybe he might be open to hearing the truth if his guard isn't quite so high.

Rubbing my thumb over his, I say, "Michael told me something else while we talked downstairs."

He glances my way. "He did? What did he say?"

I take a breath and plunge on. "He said that Fate was being meddlesome, but that he wasn't lying. You are the Master Corvus."

His fingers flex against mine and the car lurches forward, suddenly accelerating. "The Corvus inside me would know if he was the Master Corvus."

I watch the speedometer climb to eighty, then eighty-five. "Ethan, please slow down."

His hand cinches tight around my fingers. "It's *not* true," he says, raising his voice.

I yank my hand from his and yell, "Slow down, right now!"

Ethan shakes his head and blinks as if he's shocked to hear me scream at him. Finally his foot eases on the pedal. We both breathe heavily and stare at the windshield.

After several minutes of silence, he says, "I'm sorry I scared you, but what you're saying can't possibly be true. I would've known that Danielle lied to me and that she'd gone dark. I would've known that I created all the other Corvus out there. I would've known where they're located. I would've known what happened in the past with the Order—"

"That's just it, Ethan. Something happened thirty years ago. Something contributed to the Master Corvus forgetting who he is."

"But if I'm the Master Corvus, that means I'm solely responsible for all the Furiae that have been created."

And with that last, regretful comment, I realize why he's so freaked out. Only Ethan would completely ignore the implication that being the Master Corvus means he'll have to face and fight Lucifer—a realization that terrifies me. No, instead he's reacting with supreme guilt.

I reach for his hand and fold my fingers around his.

"Ethan, *you* aren't the Master Corvus. *You* didn't forget who you are. The spirit did. *You* didn't create the Furiae. My guess is they've risen in numbers over the past thirty years because he's forgotten and is running purely on instinct."

"It doesn't change the fact I might've created some over the past couple of months, Nara," he says, his hand going slack against mine. "So yeah, I've contributed. And right now the Corvus is inside me screaming 'hell no'. I can't hear him, but I feel his furious denial, his rage and his utter resentment over the suggestion. He doesn't believe it. He trusts no one."

"Not even me?" I say, sadness making my heart ache.

Ethan doesn't answer at first, but then he squeezes my fingers, his tone softening. "He doesn't trust your source."

My eyes widen. "He doesn't trust Michael?"

Ethan's jaw muscle jumps. "Not anyone. Don't ask me how I know. I just do." Staring straight ahead, he murmurs, "I wish I could talk to Michael myself—to see what angle he's playing, but I can't even see the archangel."

A few seconds pass, as if he's working through something while he drives, then his focus snaps to me. "What is this job Michael expects you to do?"

I take a breath and gesture toward him. "He wants me to help the Master Corvus remember."

An utter stillness sweeps across his expression right before he pulls away and sets both hands on the steering wheel, tension stiffening his shoulders. "So, I'm an assignment?"

"Of course not. I was just answering your question as to what Michael had to say about the Master Corvus. If you ask, I will always tell you the truth, Ethan. That's a promise we made to each other. Remember?"

"Why didn't you tell me what he said this morning?"

I gesture to him. "Look at your reaction. You were

worked up this morning. I waited until I thought you were in a better frame of mind."

He shrugs as if my response doesn't matter, like he'd already made up his own mind about my motivations.

Great. This is turning into one of those "I can't win" moments.

"I hope you don't mind if I just drop you by your car, then go. I don't want to be late picking Samson up."

I check the clock on my phone. He has plenty of time to pick up his brother. I open my mouth to call him on it, but instead I just nod. Maybe he needs some time alone. "Whatever works best for you." I can tell I've shocked him. He reacted exactly like I thought he would, which makes me glad I'd waited to tell him. This morning would've been a disaster.

I glance over his profile, his face now a mask of impassiveness, and wonder how much of his reaction is the Corvus inside him, protesting with every spiritual fiber of his being. Then again, if the spirit suddenly believed he *was* capable of the Master Corvus' powers right after he got this news, I'm not so sure I'd want to be within blast radius. Maybe I should count myself lucky the raven spirit inside him is even more stubborn than Ethan.

Staring out the window at the burgeoning clouds threatening more snow, I wonder all over again what Michael saw in me all those years ago. Why does he think I'm the perfect person to lead the Master Corvus back to himself? So far I really suck at this job.

CHAPTER 4

NARA

After Ethan dropped me off, I ran some Christmas errands, then decided to do something constructive instead of going home and stewing in frustration.

I drove straight to the cemetery.

The blanket of snow over Freddie's grave made it harder to find right away, but I finally managed to dig up the book on ravens I'd buried there for safekeeping.

I plan to scour the book tonight once more on my own, then I'll call Ethan over to look at it with me tomorrow. I know he needs some time to sort the Master Corvus stuff out in his head. Hopefully by then, he'll be in a better frame of mind to help me try to figure out how the book ties into my role.

My gut tells me there's more to it than Michael has let on. One thing's for sure; at least one demon is still out there looking for this book with the belief it holds the key to killing the Master Corvus—something Lucifer would definitely want to possess if it's true.

So far I haven't noticed any more disturbed snow around the tree outside my window. The snow had already filled in where the demon who'd kidnapped me—well, Drystan, who'd been possessed by the demon at the time—had tried and failed to find Freddie's book there, which is where I told him I'd hidden it. Thoughts of Drystan with his spiked mess of blond-streaked, light-brown hair and teasing smile flash through my mind. After everything that happened, I'm thankful we said goodbye on good terms.

Nara?

I jerk my head around, my fingers clutching the steering wheel tight. The voice echoing in my head had an accent that sounded just like…"Drystan?" I whisper. Nothing. Shaking my head, I sigh, knowing I conjured up his Welsh lilt calling my name.

Did Drystan make it to London okay? Is he settling into his new life? Is he going to join his uncle's group, the Order, and play a Paladin support role to a Corvus? Now that he's probably already seen the Order's headquarters in London, I have so many questions I want to ask him. Hopefully I'll hear from him soon.

The sudden trilling on my phone, its ring tone telling me it's someone I don't know, grabs my attention. I quickly answer, snickering at the idea that my thoughts could've prompted Drystan to call with his new contact information like he'd promised before he left.

"Hello?"

"Nara? It's David."

"Oh, hey…" I'm a bit thrown that he's calling me. It still feels awkward not calling him Mr. Dixon like I do in Spanish class, but for Mom's sake, I make the effort. "David. Are you and Mom all done with the decorations?"

"Yep, we finished up a couple hours ago. Actually, that's why I'm calling. Are you home?"

"No, but I'll be there in about ten minutes. Why?"

"While your Mom's out grocery shopping for Christmas

Eve's dinner tomorrow night, would you mind if I stopped by to drop her present off? It's a bulky box and I'd rather hide it at your house than bring it in with me tomorrow night. I can be there not long after you get home."

"Sure. No problem. See you in a bit."

Houdini nudges his big head against my thigh as I walk into the kitchen from the garage. I'm kind of relieved Mom's not home right now. I know we need to talk about Dad, but right now my nerves are wound pretty tight over Ethan/Corvus stuff.

I set my phone on the island, then lay the bundle of mistletoe on top of Freddie's book. After Mr. Dixon leaves, I'll put the book away and hang the mistletoe. The last thing I want is for my teacher to assume the mistletoe is for him and my mom. Ugh.

I shake my head and take in the over-the-top decorated tree, and the holly and red ribbon adorning every bit of shelf space in the living room. The tree might be fake, but now I smell pine. Yep, Mom's even put in a wall plug-in that's spritzing the scent each time I move into its motion detector range. I step back out of its path to stand between the kitchen and the living room. Houdini sneezes then leans against my thigh. Rubbing my thumb on the soft spot between his eyes and down along his nose, I murmur, "Don't worry. That plug-in's magically disappearing tonight."

When my dog's only response is to tilt his head like he's desperately trying to understand me, I smile. "Never mind. Do you want to go out?" His ears jump up, right before he bounds to the front door. I laugh and grab his leash from the coatrack. "Come on. We may as well take care of this before Mr. Dixon gets here."

The moment I open the front door, Houdini jerks out of my hand before I can attach the leash to his collar. I call to him to stop, but this time he pins his ears to the side of his head and bolts after two rabbits. Tufts of snow kick up behind his big paws as he darts around the side of our house. A moment of worry sets in, but it's freezing out, and Houdini has never taken off from my yard before when he's been let off the leash. He'll be back before too long. Sighing, I start to close the door when Mr. Dixon's car pulls into the driveway.

I wait while Mr. Dixon unfolds his tall, lanky frame from his car, then carries a wrapped box the size of a small microwave up the walkway to our door.

"That's definitely bigger than a breadbasket," I tease, eyeing the huge white bow on top of the red box.

The brisk air ruffles his short hair as he shifts the box in his arms. "Yeah, it's a bit awkward."

Stepping out of the doorway, I gesture toward the tree. "You can put it under there."

He follows me inside. "I was hoping I could hide it. Your mom might guess what's in the box. I want to surprise her."

I shut the door and stare at the box. "What is it?"

"A crock pot," he says, a hint of a smirk tilting his lips.

I hold back an instant desire to snicker at such a strange gift. Clearing my throat, I keep my face as straight as possible. "Oh, I don't think she'd guess that in a million years."

He shrugs, his amusement melting into a smile. "There's another gift inside—that's the best part of the present. I want her to be surprised, so yeah, I'd like to hide it. Maybe in your garage behind a storage box on the shelves?"

I lift my hand toward the garage door in the kitchen. "Go for it."

I follow him out to the garage and pull down a big plastic storage box to hide the gift behind. Once he places the gift on the shelf, I slide the box back into place, covering it up.

As we enter the kitchen once more, he asks, "Can I get a

glass of water, Nara? Been running around all morning and haven't even had time for lunch."

"Sure." I turn from pulling down a glass to see Mr. Dixon's standing there with a butcher knife in his hand and murderous intent in his eyes.

The glass shatters across the floor, but before I can take more than one step, he rushes me. Shoving me against the counter, he presses the sharp edge of the knife against the side of my throat.

I instinctively claw his hand, trying to pull the knife away, but he's just too strong. He doesn't budge. As pinpricks of pain radiate from my neck and fear shoots through me, my phone starts to ring on the counter. Ethan's ringtone. He must sense I'm in danger. My phone continues to ring and ring.

"No one's going to help you. Least of all that Corvus. I've made sure to let some of Lucifer's demons know there's a Corvus here in town. They'll be coming after him soon enough." David's voice is harsh and grating, so unlike his usual pleasant one." When my eyes snap to his, his tone turns almost conversational. "It's been a while. What did the demon call you that night at the school?" David tilts his head, sifting through memories, then gives me a cold smile. "Ah, yes, little bird."

As soon as he says "little bird" I know which demon has possessed my mother's boyfriend; the same demon that took over an evil guy named Drake so he could attack me during the school dance. All because the demon wanted Freddie's book.

My heart beats harder. I keep my attention on him and hope the mistletoe I set on the book is completely covering its blue edges.

Only this can't be him, can it? I shake my head in confusion. "He...he obliterated you that night. I saw it happen.

You're supposed to be gone..." I trail off when another option occurs.

David's face contorts in anger. "Being jabbed by that Corvus' sword hurt like a motherfucker, but he didn't just send the Lucifer demon—that Inferi—who'd taken over my body to Under. Your boyfriend's sword also separated my soul from my body when he killed me, allowing *me* to take over any body I want now." He glances down at Mr. Dixon's hand fisted around the knife, then pushes the blade even closer. "Your teacher getting it on with your mom gave me perfect access. I just had to wait until that other Inferi stopped sniffing around here before I slipped into good old David's lanky frame. Who knows...maybe I'll stick around and see if your mom is cougar material."

"Don't even think of going near her," I say, baring my teeth at the demon.

He chuckles, then the pain in my neck sharpens and a slight metallic taste fills my mouth. I'd been right about the other option; during their fight at the school dance, Ethan's sword had sent the Inferi inside Drake's body back to Under. But apparently Drake had been possessed too long by a Lucifer demon and his human soul had been fully corrupted. Ethan's sword had killed Drake, turning his soul into a Furia—a single demon bound to Lucifer's will and doomed to roam the Mortal world.

My fingers dig at David's wrist, and I try once more to pull the knife away from my throat. This time, when I tighten my fingers and grip his skin, David glances at my hand in annoyance, noticing my hold on him for the first time.

"Stop screwing around!" he bites out. "I want that raven book you stole from me. And you're going to tell me where it is. *Right now.*"

I jump when Houdini throws himself against the front

door. Vicious snarls and frenzied defense mode barking alternate between scratches on the door. He smells the demon in our house.

During a split second of silence, a text comes through on my phone, drawing my attention. The second David follows my line of sight, instant recognition of the book's edge underneath the mistletoe sparks in his eyes.

Laughing, he lowers the knife and leans over to push the plant out of the way, but his hand just stops. It's like he's hitting an invisible wall and a force field is protecting the plant. Even when he tries to use the knife instead, the knife diverts away. He can't touch it.

Exhaling a breath of relief, I start to skirt past him, but he yanks my arm and shoves me against the island, his fingers digging into my skin painfully. "It must be the plant. Remove it."

I lift my chin high. "You killed an innocent old man just to get that book. I'll never give it to you."

He snarls and sets the knife back against my throat. "Now, Nara!"

I try not to think about the stinging pain and shake my head as I grip his wrist, squeezing tight. David hisses, then slits his eyes and flexes his wrist, the blade applying pressure to my neck once more. "That book can elevate me much higher in Lucifer's domain. He might even allow me entrance into Under as one of *his* demons in payment for bringing it to him."

When a trickle of warm blood slides down my chest, my stomach roils with nausea. "You can't have it," I say, cinching my fingers like a vise around his arm.

An eerie growl rumbles from deep in his chest. "I have no issue slitting your throat and leaving you to die choking on your own blood if you don't hand it over—"

David's focus narrows on my hand on his wrist. Hatred

flares in his eyes right before a foul smell quickly fills my nostrils.

As I fight the need to gag and wonder if the horrible odor is his demon stench, he dips his head and the blade against my neck slackens while he takes several deep breaths. At the same time I realize David's fighting the demon inside him, my brain identifies the awful smell: burning flesh. The raven yin-yang symbol on my ring meant to protect me from demon possession (of the Furia or Inferi variety) must be pressing against his wrist.

A rumble of rage erupts from the Furia right before his attention swings back to mine, full of cruel and lethal intent. While the knife twitches torturously against my neck, I flatten my free hand on David's chest and stare into his eyes. "Fight him, David!"

My palm begins to tingle with heat, and then the demon thrashes his head back and forth, shrieking like excruciating pain is flooding through him.

Horror briefly tears across Mr. Dixon's face, and the sight makes me think of Drystan. The terror he must've felt being trapped inside, a puppet to evil's every whim.

That the demon dared to mention my mother's name spikes my protective nature. Rage flares like a rumbling volcano, traveling from my belly up my chest, and then past the lump in my throat. I'm so outraged, I'm able to distance my mind from the pain the knife's inflicting. Spreading my fingers on his chest, I dig into his flesh and grit out with every ounce of will I've got, "Get out of him now!"

A flash of glaring white light shoots out of several points from David's body at the same time my expanding chest and burning lungs suddenly collapse inward in a painful exhalation. I gasp for air as my arms and legs turn to jelly, and my whole body starts to tremor. The second the light fades,

David and I both stumble back, and the knife in his hand clatters to the floor.

I take a deep, shuddering breath, then exhale my relief. I'm so drained and shaken by whatever-the-heck just happened, I have to grab the edge of the counter to keep from collapsing. Cool air hitting the blood on my neck brings both chill bumps and sharp pain, reminding me I'm hurt. I quickly grab a dishtowel to staunch my wound, while my teacher slowly shakes his head, blinking his way back to consciousness.

"Nara?" He glances around, completely confused. "When did I get here?" Wincing, he rubs his forehead. "Why is my head pounding?"

I somehow tuned out Houdini while the demon and I battled wills and my life was hanging in the balance, but now my dog's ferocious growls are all I hear. David tenses at the sound, and he takes in the broken glass and knife on the floor. He swings his eyes back to me, and his eyes widen at the trickle of blood on my chest.

"God, are you okay?" He takes a step toward me, hand raised to help. Then he pauses, unsure what to do. "What happened?"

Before I can answer, the front door flies open. Houdini and Ethan rush in. Houdini's fur is raised and his teeth are bared as he snarls and jerks his head around, looking for me. Ethan's stance is deadly, his eyes as black as sin when they lock with mine.

The moment they both bolt for the kitchen, I quickly step in front of Mr. Dixon and call out, "Broken glass!" to Ethan, then address my dog, commanding, "*Stay*, Houdini."

When Ethan grabs Houdini's collar to keep him back, I nod my thanks and speak to him in a calm, but firm tone, "Mr. Dixon just had a blackout episode, but he's okay now."

"What?" Ethan's staring at me like I've lost my mind. He

directs my dog to sit, but Ethan's stance remains battle-ready, his eyes darting suspiciously to Mr. Dixon behind me. "Let me talk to him, Nara."

"He's good, Ethan. Trust me."

"I—I don't even know what's going on. Or how I got here." Mr. Dixon blows out an unsteady breath, then gestures toward my neck. "Or why you're bleeding, Nara. Please tell me I didn't do that?"

"No." I turn to him. "It was an accident. It happened when you blacked out. We'd just finished hiding Mom's present in the garage and then came back into the kitchen when you started stumbling all over the place. It's like you were sleep-walking or something. You grabbed a knife and kept saying there's an intruder in our house."

He pales, dread in his eyes. "So I did hurt you."

I shake my head in fast jerks. "Not on purpose. I don't blame you at all, David. When I raised my voice, you snapped out of it. Like you woke up. Don't worry, I won't tell Mom. But maybe you should go home and get some rest. You look exhausted."

"I've never slept-walked in my life," he murmurs in confusion, glancing down at the glass all over the floor. "I'll stay and help you clean this up."

He's visibly shaking and his voice is hoarse. I can't imagine what it must feel like to lose a period of time and then wake up to bloody chaos and mayhem all around you. I'd be freaked out too. "Ethan will help me. You should go home. Mom will be back soon. You don't want to spoil the surprise for her. Don't worry, David. Honestly, everything's fine now."

When Mr. Dixon mumbles more apologies and then starts to get upset all over again, I turn imploring eyes to Ethan and mouth, "Please help him."

He sighs and steps forward to grip Mr. Dixon on the

shoulder. "I'm sure you'll feel better after you get some sleep. Maybe you blacked out because you aren't getting enough rest."

Ethan's calming touch works, and David inhales and exhales slowly, nodding. "I slept eight hours last night, but for some strange reason I do feel extremely tired."

Once Ethan walks Mr. Dixon out, I rush to the bathroom to grab the first-aid kit and see how much damage Drake's demon did to my neck.

Staring in the mirror, I sigh with relief that the wound is only a couple inches long and doesn't appear deep enough for stitches. An emergency room visit would be much harder to hide from my mom.

Houdini sits right outside the bathroom doorway and whines. I glance his way. "It's okay, boy. I'm fine."

Ethan enters the bathroom, his face unreadable. He reaches for the alcohol swab in my hand. "Let me do it."

His voice is even, but his eyes are still mostly black and very little blue. He needs to calm down as much as I do. I release the swab and nod, tilting my chin up. The second the wet cotton hits my cut, I wince.

Ethan tenses, but doesn't talk while he cleanses my wound and washes the blood off my chest. While he attaches a bandage to my neck, his voice is gruff. "You're going to need to wear something to cover this up until it heals."

"I know," I say quietly.

Ethan cups the back of my neck, his thumb gently rubbing the side of my throat. "Was he looking for the book?"

I nod.

His brows pull together in a deep frown.

"He almost got it too. I'd just returned from retrieving it and brought it in the house. Mr. Dixon called about Mom's present and got here before I could hide it." My lips quirk.

"The mistletoe I'd set on top of it kept the demon from touching it."

More blue takes over the black in Ethan's eyes and he smiles. "Told you it had protective properties." Sobering, he continues, "I'm glad you're okay. Samson and I were on the other side of town when my body started to buzz with worry. I knew you were in trouble. I left my brother to finish his errand, so I can't stay long. I need to go pick him up."

Touching my chin, he tilts it until our eyes lock. "The crazed way Houdini was acting when I got here told me a demon was inside, but I didn't smell anything once we came in." His forehead creases in confusion. "Even if the demon had left David's body, I usually still smell its trace in the air for a while, but this time I didn't. How is that possible?"

My voice shakes as I tell Ethan everything that happened. When I finish, he grasps my shoulders gently, a look of wonder on his face. "You expelled a demon from Mr. Dixon with just your touch? That's *amazing*."

I purse my lips in a rueful half smile. "I have no idea if that's what I did or even how I did it. I just really wanted that demon out of David."

Ethan looks thoughtful. "Every demon I've expelled with my sword bursts out of the person's body in a pale yellow mist. That's been true whether it was an Inferi or a Furia. The fact that you saw a flash of light shoot out of him instead of yellow mist has to mean something else."

"I have no idea what it means." I run my teeth across my bottom lip, then stop when the slight flexing of my neck muscles pulls on my wound.

"Unless…" He tilts his head.

"Unless what?"

Stepping into the hallway, Ethan sniffs toward the kitchen. "I can't smell even the smallest trace of the demon. It's like it was never here."

I follow him into the hall. "What are you thinking?"

"Are you *sure* you're not an angel?"

I spread my hands wide. "I think that's something Michael would've mentioned. Why?"

Ethan rubs his jaw. "If that was a Furia demon—"

"It was."

"How do you know?"

"Drake's soul took over David's body," I say.

Guilt scrolls across Ethan's face. I know he's thinking about the fact he's the one who created the Furia inside David. Then hope brightens his eyes. "I wonder if…you just *freed* Drake's soul from Lucifer's influence."

"You think his soul's no longer Furia?" I nod, thinking it through. "That would explain me seeing something different leave his body, and it would also explain why you can't smell anything. Both you and Houdini have always been able to in the past."

He nods, smiling broadly. "There has definitely got to be some angel in you."

I snort and shake my head. "I'm just glad Mr. Dixon's okay. Do you think he bought the sleep-walking story?"

"What choice does he have? It's either that or think he's gone crazy. For his own peace of mind, I hope he does believe it." Lifting his chin toward the front door, Ethan continues, "Once I leave, put the mistletoe up over all the entrances to your house. Hanging them in the doorways will add a layer of protection against demons. Unfortunately there isn't a permanent way to safe-guard your house against them, but the mistletoe should last for a few days until it dries out."

Houdini whimpering and pawing at his ear snags my attention. "What's wrong, boy?" When he licks his paw, I notice the blood on it. "What happened?" I step close and squat to lift his paw so I can check for an injury.

"It's his ear," Ethan says, touching Houdini's floppy right ear.

I glance up at the wound along the tip and frown. "It's sliced open. Poor guy."

Once I return from the bathroom with a clean alcohol swab for Houdini, Ethan's face is stony, his tone laced with anger. "It looks like someone took a pair of scissors and snipped the edge of his ear."

His vivid imagery makes my stomach twinge. "Can you hold his collar while I clean his wound? This is going to hurt."

After I clean the wound and rig the bandage into a butterfly-type suture to hopefully help the cut heal back together, I stand and glance into the kitchen. "I'd better get that glass cleaned up before Mom gets home."

As I turn to walk away, Ethan reaches for my hand. Threading our fingers together, he says, "I'm sorry about earlier in the car." He swallows. "I just don't know what to think about all this Corvus stuff."

He won't even use the term "Master Corvus." I squeeze his hand. "I know. You haven't mentioned the scariest part. The thought that you might have to fight Lucifer worries me more than anything."

He shrugs. "That's only if it's true. I'm still in the 'I don't believe it' camp."

I *wish* it wasn't true, but no amount of wishing or ignoring can change reality. "Stubborn," I say, sighing heavily. "Go pick up your brother. Come by later and we'll go over Freddie's book."

Ethan nods, then turns to retrieve my zip-up hoodie from the coatrack. He holds it up for me and I slide my arms into it.

Once I zip it all the way, he rests his hands lightly on my shoulders, his eyes flicking to the gauze on my neck the jacket had just covered up. "That was entirely too close, Nara. We have to figure out the truth behind the book quickly. If we can't, we don't have a choice. We'll have to destroy it too."

The thought of destroying any book yanks at my heart—anyone who loves to read would feel the same. But this particular book has been protected for so long, the idea of turning it to ash to protect its secrets twinges at my heart even more. "At least we don't have to worry about Drake anymore," I say in a light tone to keep from dwelling on it.

Ethan doesn't even crack a smile. "You're forgetting that Drystan's demon is still out there."

I haven't forgotten, but I frown that he's assigning Drystan's name to that Inferi. It's not like my friend chose to be possessed. If we have to give the demon a name, it should be the last person who *welcomed* its possession. "For whatever reason *Harper's* Inferi is laying low for now." Then I remember what Drake's Furia said, and I put a hand on Ethan's chest. "The demon told me that he let some Inferni know that you're living here in Blue Ridge, Ethan. I got the impression he didn't mention the book because he wanted that for himself. I'm assuming he wanted his revenge but knew he wasn't strong enough to fight you. Please, please keep a watch out. I can't imagine demons knowing that a Corvus is around and not going after you."

Ethan tenses his jaw. "I'm always on alert."

When he doesn't make a move to leave and his fingers flex on my shoulders, applying pressure, I know he wishes he can stay to protect me. Leaning close, I kiss his jaw. "I'll be fine. The mistletoe will go up as soon as you walk out. I have no more plans to go anywhere. Feel better?"

Nodding, he presses a warm kiss to my forehead, then closes the door behind him.

CHAPTER 5

ETHAN

*A*s I drive away from Nara's house, the gravelly voice I hadn't heard in a while rushes through my mind. *You're not worthy of her.*

I narrow my gaze. *I know who you are now, Corvus. Stop hiding behind that stupid horror film voice.*

She might've just washed away your guilt in one fell swoop, but you'll never be worthy.

The Corvus had switched his voice to a deep bass one, full of authority and judgment, but at least he didn't sound like some haggard creeper any more. I ignore his attempt to rile me. *How did she expel a demon with just her touch?*

It takes him a full minute to answer. *I don't know.*

I can't believe even my Corvus doesn't know. Worry ripples through me. *You've never seen this before?*

Another long pause. *No. It just highlights the fact that you don't deserve her.*

You're the one who made me go all silent on her this morning. Your volatile emotions over what Nara said about the Master Corvus could've gotten us killed if I hadn't concentrated on keeping the car on the road.

Silence.

Sometimes I really hate the bastard living inside me. I grit my teeth, then take a breath to calm down. *Why have you tortured me all this time? What was the purpose of trying to drive me crazy?*

It wasn't torture. You needed to toughen up. This body worked for me, but it needed to be stronger. You would either break or survive.

He wanted to break me? My fingers cinch on the steering wheel. I see red for several seconds, but I shake my head to keep my shit together. I need answers, and he's finally talking. *Survive? For what purpose? Are you the Master Corvus?*

Don't believe the bullshit that lowly angel *is feeding Nara.*

Why didn't I automatically know how to fight demons then? Shouldn't that have come with your invasion *of my body?* I finish, curling my lip in a snarl.

If you hadn't resisted my presence all this time, the calling of your sword and all that entails would've been intuitive. I told you that you didn't want to know me. But now that you know, stop fighting my existence and let me take over completely.

Screw that, Corvus. This is my body. My mind. My life *you're fucking with.*

An arrogant grunt rushes through my mind. *Not any more it's not. Only one other was this resistant. Though his mind wasn't quite as layered as yours.*

I can't tell if that's respect in his tone or annoyance. *Let me guess. Adder?*

Silence.

I clench my jaw and command, *Tell me about him.* When the spirit stays quiet, I fist my hand in my lap. Had he screwed with Adder's head like he did with mine? *You tried to make me kill myself, you twisted bastard.*

You were mixing your dreams and reality. You'd already crossed paths with several demons and with so much dark energy swirling in you, all that converged and your mind started to splinter. Thought I'd see if I could help you break it, but somehow you managed not to go insane.

His blasé, condescending attitude makes me seethe. I lock my jaw and try to keep my thoughts focused, when all I want to do is curse him for everything he'd put me through. *I want you* gone!

Too bad. You're the perfect vessel. I will always be here.

My fist flexes on the steering wheel. I pin my focus on the road. *Tell me what I need to know about demons. All of it.*

When the spirit doesn't reply, renewed anger whips through me, quickly followed by dogged determination. Maybe going on the offensive might get the arrogant prick to talk. *Why don't you know more about being a Corvus? Are you a reject, the runt of your Papa Corvus' litter?* I add another jab just to piss him off. *Am I infested with damaged goods?*

Watch your mouth, you worthless bit of insignificant flesh, the Corvus snarls, his voice sounding more old-world and bolder, building in bullish fury. My head suddenly throbs and my chest actually expands, my ribs creaking and my lungs burning like they're going to burst any moment.

I take shallow breaths to try to calm the storm swirling inside me, but then my foot slams down on the pedal. Just like it did this morning. I try to pull my toe up, but I can't. As I watch the speedometer vault upward, a rush of adrenaline spikes within, and I find that place in my head I've gone many times before.

I jerk my head up and a cold, confident smile tilts my lips. *You* need *this worthless bit of flesh, asshole.* With my car moving at racecar speed, I'm glad I'm on the open highway and Nara's not here to freak out. This battle is between me and this self-important prick. He's not making me back down.

I am *Corvus*. His voice grates in a superior boom.

The car shudders. Wind buffets the doors and hood under the climbing speed. I grip the wheel and focus on keeping the car on the road. *You haven't shared any Corvus stuff with me. Why is Adder's talent the only one I seem to know like it's my own?*

Just as the speedometer hits one-fifteen, the pressure on my foot loosens and he answers, *Stop being stubborn and refusing to accept me. You'll soon learn I'm equally obstinate.*

I bark out a harsh laugh. *Then find someone with less of a backbone.* A few minutes later, I slow down to turn into the hardware store's parking lot. Parking, I shut the engine off. *I'll be happy to see you gone.*

No one else comes with Nara.

I freeze in the process of opening my car door. My fingers dig into the handle, the hard piece creaking under my hold as a cold chill slides down my back. *What the hell does that mean?*

Silence.

She is mine, you egotistical, oversized bird. I don't like that he's not answering. *Stay the hell away from her.*

His throaty, assured laugh floats through my head. *Can you?*

A territorial growl erupts from my lips. *She is not, nor will she ever be* yours.

You are unworthy, he says.

Rage builds inside me. I'm about to let loose all the obscenities I've been holding back, when he says, *We both are.*

He sounded resigned to that fact. I'm silent as I walk inside the hardware store. At least that's one thing we both agree on. *I love her,* I say, subdued by his honesty.

Her lightness is addictive. I don't reply. I'm not even sure if that last comment was the Corvus' thought or mine. One thing I know for certain; I have to learn how to block him from listening in, from reacting, and from fucking taking over.

You can't keep her from me, the Corvus says, his tone building in conceited assurance. *Her light always finds a way through.*

His smugness sends a jolt of jealousy ripping straight through me, gnawing at my gut. Nara says he's a spirit, but she doesn't know he's the one who sped up my car this morning. The fact he can take over against my will infuriates and terrifies me. He's put Nara at risk before when he pulled her into my dreams so she could face down Fate against her father. I refuse to let him do it again. Ignoring his last comment, I turn a corner to head down the aisle where I'd left Samson browsing.

With two books in one arm and a third in his other hand, my brother lifts his blond head. "It's a good thing I take forever to decide. Is Nara okay? You went really pale." He pauses and stares at me oddly. "I've never seen you move so fast."

Apparently I'd been too freaked out over Nara's safety to keep my Corvus speed in check. I shove my hands in my jean pockets and nod, keeping my tone low-key. "She's good. Someone tried to break into her house recently, so I worry about her even with the new security system."

As I skim over the do-it-yourself home improvement books and magazines lining the shelves in front of my brother, an idea sparks and I give the Corvus a final warning. *If you don't stay the hell out of my head and out of my way, I'll find a way to shut you up permanently.*

There has got to be books on mental exercises I can try that'll help me learn to block him from my mind. After I drop Samson off at home, I'll head to the bookstore, then finish my Christmas shopping. There's just one more purchase I hadn't anticipated having to make so soon, but at least I found a place that can handle last minute requests.

CHAPTER 6

NARA

I'm in the process of hanging the last piece of mistletoe over the kitchen doorway when the bay garage door begins to open. Houdini raises his head from his bed in the living room and barks once, but I tell him to settle and scramble off the stepladder to put it away.

Heart racing, I pick up the bloody knife from the floor, rinse it off in the sink, then slide it into the dishwasher rack.

My hands shake as I retrieve the dustpan and broom, but I tell myself to stay focused on my task. A fine sheen of sweat coats my face while I frantically try to sweep up all the pieces of broken glass. The glass makes *chink-chink* sounds, sliding off the pan into the trash a split-second before the kitchen door opens.

"You're cleaning?" Mom says in surprise as she walks in carrying two big bags of groceries.

I push the trashcan into the closet, then set the hand broom and dustpan back under the sink. "I *do* do that every once in a while without being asked."

Mom raises her eyebrow and I smile. At least we're talking. "Need some help?"

"Yes, there are two more bags in my car."

As Mom and I unload the groceries, I'm surprised to see a roast. "You're making pot roast?" I ask, setting the meat in the fridge.

Mom puts the potatoes, carrots and celery into the crisper. Sliding the bin shut, she says, "I thought we'd try something different."

"The pine scent plug-in wasn't enough?"

Houdini walking into the kitchen sets the thing off, and a spritz of strong pine fills the air.

Mom's brow creases. "Too much?"

Houdini sneezes three times, and they're wet sneezes too. I snicker at the look of disgust on Mom's face before she quickly moves to the wall and unplugs the unit.

I pat Houdini on the head, murmuring, "It's okay now, boy. The torture is over."

A worried look crosses Mom's face. "What happened to Houdini's ear?"

"I don't know. He took off after those rabbits, and it was torn when he came back."

Mom frowns. "Keep an eye on it and keep it clean. The vet might need to see it."

"I will."

Setting the plugin on the counter, Mom sighs. "I was just trying to make it a Christmas to remember."

"It will be, Mom. We're celebrating it together. That's all that matters."

She gives me a genuine smile for the first time since this morning. I smile back and grab an empty paper bag off the counter. The whole thing with Drake's demon earlier could've gone in a very bad direction. What if something had happened to me before I could tell Mom about Dad? Would she believe him without me around to prove that his ability did exist back then? Mom needs to know the truth. I begin to fold the bag into itself and say, "We need to talk about this morning."

Mom had started to fold another bag on the other side of the island. She stops folding and meets my gaze, tension in her grip on the brown paper. "How long have you been talking to your father, Inara?"

"Yesterday was only the second day I've talked to him."

Her face relaxes a little. "Did he contact you?"

"Yes," I answer honestly. "But technically he only contacted me to warn me."

"Warn you?" Mom's eyes widen in alarm. "About what?"

I set the bag down and move around the island to stand in front of her. "I want to talk to you about him."

Her lips press together and she jerks her head back and forth. "I don't want to discuss your father, Inara. We were talking about you."

"But this *is* about me, Mom. And it's about Dad and what he talked to me about."

"What do you mean?"

"Dad…has this ability."

"Oh, that?" Mom waves her hand. "I already know."

Disbelief rolls through me. "You do?"

Grabbing the bag I hadn't finished folding, she folds it. She turns around and slides it beside the others under the sink, then says, "I knew he had some kind of gift, but I wasn't sure how it worked."

I blink several times. I can't believe it. All this time…she knew? "Why didn't you ask him about it?"

Mom shrugs. "It didn't matter to me. And honestly, I didn't want to know. It's not like I could share the experience with him."

"But you could've made him feel like he was normal, regardless." *Or at least made me feel that way.*

She sets her hands on her hips, her face creasing in defensive lines. "Are you implying that your father leaving is my fault? That's what you're leading up to, right? You're going to tell me why he left?"

"Dad didn't blame you. At all."

"Well, he shouldn't have! He's the one who took off without a word, remember?"

"I don't need a reminder, Mom," I say, adopting her defensive tone.

When her back stiffens, I take a deep breath to try to calm myself. "Actually, I was going to show you some videos he left for me, instead. I think they'll help you understand better."

She clamps her lips together for a second. "I don't want to see them."

"Why?"

Mom unbuttons her jacket and takes it off. She's getting ready to go upstairs and change into more comfortable clothes...and also end our conversation. The fact she's preparing to walk away ticks me off. "I can't believe you've known all along that Dad had an ability." I'm shaking so hard I have to grab the counter to steady myself.

"Inara, why are you so upset?"

"Because *I* developed the same ability and had to go through it alone, Mom. I didn't tell you because I thought you wouldn't understand. That you might think I was a freak. Why in the world would you intentionally keep that peace of mind from me?"

Tears start to trickle down her cheeks as I'm spewing out my anger.

Mom walks over and cups my face. "Oh, sweetheart. When I saw some of your father's tendencies starting to shine through not long after you started elementary school, I did try to talk to you about it."

I shake my head. "No, you didn't."

Her gaze searches mine. "Yes, I did. I tried to tell you that you were special, and you got very upset with me. You didn't want to be different. You didn't like that I pointed it out."

I blink at her a couple of times. "I did?"

She nods. "I think the last thing you wanted to hear is that you weren't the same as other kids, so I didn't say anything else about it. When you grew older, you were just so together and self-assured, I thought I'd made the right decision."

"That's because I had to be." *I thought I was all alone.* "I didn't have anyone to confide in. No one that understood."

"I'm so sorry. I had no idea." Mom offers a sad smile. "Though I don't know how much good I would've been to you. I never really could've understood, because I'm just plain old me. No special abilities here."

I snort at the utter incongruity of our viewpoints. We're like opposite ends of a magnet finally brought together but unable to align. I'm still hurt that she chose not to ask me about it once I grew up. Apparently we both should've been more open with our thoughts. "Maybe now that you're not afraid to discuss it, you can talk to Dad—"

"Afraid?" She shakes her head. "I was never afraid."

I throw my hands out. "The point is you didn't ask Dad about it. You didn't want to know. And I can tell by your expression that you still don't. Don't you understand that I needed you and you weren't there?"

"I said I'm sorry—" She goes still and her shoulders stiffen. "Are you trying to say your father left because of his ability? And you blame me for not asking him about it?"

"I'm not blaming you for Dad, at all, but I do think you should've asked. He left because he had to. Not because he wanted to. Nothing you said would've changed that."

Mom pales slightly, like that's the last thing she wanted to hear, then her face settles in determined lines. "No, Inara. He *could've* stayed. If he left because of his ability, he should've trusted me enough to tell me about it. The fact that he never did is the very reason I don't want to see those videos. Whatever that truth was, *he* should've shared it. Nothing can change that he didn't trust in our love enough to weather the storm."

It wasn't just about you. It was about keeping me safe too. I open my mouth to say this, but then I close it. Her last comments are eerily similar to the things I said to Ethan about us working together as a team; at least the underlying gist of trust and partnership is the same. I guess I'm more like her than I realize.

Ethan thanking me this morning for trusting him enough to go into that icy water pops into my head. Mom and Dad must get to that level of trust. Somehow they need to find common ground. I'm not really sure what I want for my parents. They've been apart for so long, I don't know if they're the same people they once were, but I want to give them a chance to find out if they still belong together. I want the one thing that kept them apart, my father's ability, laid in front of Mom so she can't ignore it anymore. Granted, Mom doesn't know all the facts yet, nor is she ready to hear them either, but as I've seen with Ethan, an open mind can be the key to an open heart.

Maybe instead of discussing the past with her, I should focus on the present. "You don't want to talk about past stuff, fine. Let's talk about dinner tomorrow night. I'd like Ethan to come." Once Mom nods, I continue, "And Dad too."

Her face hardens and she folds her arms. "Absolutely *not*."

"Gran's coming, and you've already invited Aunt Sage."

When she doesn't say anything, I add, "Dad's staying with his sister."

Mom shrugs. "Now that he's here, I'm assuming she'll cancel."

"It's tomorrow night. She knows you need to buy food to prepare. Has she cancelled yet?"

An uncomfortable look flashes in my mom's blue eyes. "No, she hasn't."

"It's not like you can un-invite her." I shift my tone slightly, softening it. "He'll be all alone, Mom."

She stiffens. "Whose fault is that?"

I start to say it would be the right thing to do when she suddenly tilts her head and says, "You know what…why not?" Thoughts trickle across her face like a scrolling neon sign: defiance, inspiration, then smugness. "I'll call her myself."

I realize too late exactly what Mom's new angle is. David will be here too. She wants Dad to see she's moved on. Ugh, I didn't think about how this might possibly be awkward for my teacher or create a tense environment at dinner. I open my mouth to backpedal on my request, then clamp my lips shut. The most I can hope for with this Christmas Eve dinner is to see my mom interacting with my dad again after all these years, even if it's just dinner conversation. Hopefully Mr. Dixon will take being Mom's buffer and ego booster in stride.

Right now, I *really* miss my ability to see my whole day. I have no idea how this is going to turn out. One thing's for sure, this Christmas Eve dinner won't be like *any* of our past ones.

CHAPTER 7

NARA

*W*ith time to kill before Ethan returns, I head to my room to clean it. I'd already taken care of the bathroom, but the rest needed a major reorganization.

An hour later, I unzip my jacket and set it on the bed, then open my window to cool off a little. I'd just pulled Freddie's book from under my mattress, then sat down at the desk to look over it, when Patch swoops into my room, his strong wings gliding him inside.

I gasp at his surprise entrance at the same time Houdini lifts his head from his slumber at the end of my bed. My dog's big brown eyes go wide and he instantly jumps down, then bolts out the door, his ears tucked to his head, an alarm bark trailing behind him.

"What was that all about—?" I start to ask Patch once he lands on my bed. I pause when the bird snaps his hard beak together three times toward the open doorway, then makes an annoyed huffing sound.

My gaze shifts from Patch to the doorway, then back to the massive raven walking around on my comforter, and it hits me what happened. Houdini's wound is about the size of the tip of a raven's beak. Patch must've gone after him for deserting his post to chase rabbits. The bird has always had a keen sense when I'm in danger.

Poor Houdini. "Did you have to slice his ear open? Kind of harsh, don't you think?" I gently reprimand the bird.

Patch bobs his head, then lets out a low *gronk* before flying over to land on my desk.

I keep my hands where they are on the desk, figuring it's best not to make sudden moves. Considering the way the bird came in after Houdini, he's obviously in a mood.

I can't help but curl my fingers in a little when he bends his powerful beak toward my hand. I don't even realize I'm holding my breath until he nudges his beak under my pinky, then lifts it and the finger next to it, sliding his beak and then his head under them.

Shocked, I exhale slowly and gently run my fingers across his beak, then over the silky feathers on his head. Patch tilts his head and makes a low guttural sound as he steps closer so my hand will slide down his neck.

I keep my touch light, gently rubbing his feathers. When he pushes the crown of his head against my open palm, then runs his beak along my wrist and gently clamps onto it, my heart swells with understanding. He's worried about me.

Tears blur my vision and I blink them away. "I'm okay, Patch. Everything's fine. The demon's gone."

He releases me, lifting his black eyes to mine. When he bobs his head a couple of times, I smile. "Thank you for watching over me. But please don't clip Houdini's ears any more. If he hears you coming, that should be enough to tell him to get home from now on."

Nara.

I jump and jerk my hand away from Patch, looking around my room. It's Drystan's voice again. This time I know I didn't conjure him in my mind. I'm not even thinking about him.

The video application on my open laptop beeps a couple times, drawing my attention. When I see the handle: TheWelshArse, I chuckle and click the answer button.

"Nara!"

I'm so happy to see Drystan, to know he's all right, I have to blink several times to keep from crying. "Drystan! You will not believe what just happened. Were you just thinking about me?"

He gives me a duh look. "Yeah, hence the reason for my handle."

"I just heard you—" Pausing, I squint to see the tapestries on the wall behind him. They look...old. "Where are you?"

He follows my line of sight, then looks back at me and shrugs. "Guess that gives me away. We ended up leaving early instead of waiting 'til Monday. My uncle didn't want to deal with holiday traveling."

"So you're in London now?"

"Yeah. What do you mean you heard me?"

"I heard you say my name."

He nods. "I did, right when the video popped up."

I shake my head. "No, before that—wait...are you wearing my scarf?"

He tugs on the ends he'd pulled through the loop, tightening the gray scarf around his neck. "Uh, yeah." Blowing on his hands, he rubs them together. "It's right cold in this part of the building."

I shake my head and sigh. "At least now I know where my scarf went. Been looking for it."

"Sorry 'bout that. Found it when I emptied out my sports bag. Must've picked it up along with my stuff after practice." A sheepish grin flashes. "It has come in handy here though, so thanks for the borrow. Guess you'll have to come to London to retrieve it."

He's so shamelessly cheeky, I can't help but laugh. "You keep it. It looks good on you, very European. So tell me… how is it there? Does it feel like being in Wales? Do you feel at home yet?"

"It's…London, which can never compare to Wales." He runs his hand through his light brown hair, pride for his homeland reflecting in his green eyes, but I notice his smile doesn't quite reach them.

"Something's wrong? What is it?"

The right side of his mouth quirks slightly. "You know me so well. You're the only one who does."

I lean closer to the laptop. "Tell me, Dryst."

At that moment, Patch leans in front of the screen, then lets out a loud *raaack* and tries to peck at the surface.

"Quiet, Patch," I hiss right before Mom calls upstairs.

"Nara? Why is Houdini suddenly shivering at my feet? Is he getting sick?"

"He's fine, Mom. Just got spooked over something." I look at Drystan. "Hold on a sec. I need to put the bird back outside before my dog has a heart attack."

"Come on, Patch." I wait until he climbs onto my wrist, then I walk over to my window and hold my wrist outside. "I'll see you tomorrow."

Once he's gone, I shut my window and return to my laptop. "Sorry about that. Patch is—"

"What happened to you?" Drystan suddenly tenses, a scowl pulling his brows down.

"Huh?"

"Your neck?"

He's clearly worried. My fingers instantly go to the bandage on my neck. "Oh, that. One more sec." I get up and grab my jacket. Zipping it all the way up to cover my wound, I sit back down with a sigh. "I'm fine, Drystan. Really."

"I didn't do that to you, did I?"

I quickly shake my head. "No. This was just me not being careful with my curling iron yesterday." I hate lying but he'll only worry. That's the last thing he needs right now.

"If it's bad enough that you need a bandage, maybe forget the curling iron." Exhaling, he relaxes. "I can't believe you've tamed a raven."

"Hardly. He comes and goes as he pleases."

"Why did he listen to you then?"

I shrug. "I don't know. He just does."

Drystan chuckles. "You truly are amazing."

I wave my hand. "Enough about me. What's going on with you? Are you going to join the Order?"

Drystan glances around for a second. "You should see this place, Nara. It's massive." His lips quirk. "If these walls could talk, I bet they'd have many stories to tell."

I inch closer to the laptop. "You're in the Order's sanctuary?"

"For now." He grimaces. "I'd prefer to live elsewhere, but my mum loves it here."

"So are you saying you're not going to become a Paladin to a Corvus?" The thought makes me a little sad. "No matter your differences with your uncle, the way you helped me learn to defend myself, you were born to be one, Drystan. If I were a Corvus, I'd want you to be mine."

His green eyes light up. "Yeah?"

I say softly, "Very much so."

"You'd be the only reason I'd say yes," he says, his expression darkening.

"Why? Has something happened?"

He lifts his right arm and shows me an older style wristwatch with a black leather band. "My uncle gave this to me, insisting that I wear it. My mum got a bracelet, I think."

"It has the Corvus symbol on the back, doesn't it?" I ask.

He frowns. "How'd you know?"

"Your uncle told me that he planned to give you a family heirloom with the symbol on it to protect you from demon possession."

He nods solemnly. "It felt weird when I put it on..." He pauses for a second. "I don't know how to explain it. I felt connected to it somehow."

"Keep it on, Drystan. No matter how you feel about your uncle."

His mouth curves in a mock smile. "Yeah. Well, I was in the process of looking at the Corvus symbol stamped on the back of the watch when I noticed some tool marks along the metal plate. As if someone had opened it. So I popped it open, and underneath that plate someone had manually etched DON'T TRUST."

"That sounds a bit...ominous. Did you talk to your uncle about what you found?"

"'ell no!" He huffs out, and slides his hand through his hair once more. While alternating streaks of blond and light brown flip around his fingers, his face settles. "Sorry, Nara. I didn't mean to snap. It's just...I don't trust anyone here. It's not like I can tell my mum. She doesn't even know the Order exists. You're the only person I feel safe talking to about this."

My heart twinges for him as I stare at the watch on his wrist. "It might not be as bad as you think. Yes, it could mean 'don't trust anyone,' or it could just as easily mean, 'don't trust' that the watch will protect you from demon possession. It was marked on the watch after all."

"Too late for that," he bites out.

I clamp my back teeth on the inside of my cheek, wishing

I hadn't used that example. "As far as I know, wearing the symbol on you does stop them, so definitely keep it on. Did you at least tell your uncle that you remember everything that happened while you were possessed?"

His eyes widen and his face pales. "You know that I remember?"

I dip my head, hoping understanding conveys in my expression. "Yeah, I know. I could tell by the way you were acting on Saturday night."

Rubbing the back of his neck, he glances away. "I did so many horrible things."

"That wasn't you, Drystan. It was the demon."

He rests his hands on the desk face-up in front of him and stares at his palms, his voice dropping to a hoarse whisper. "They were *my* hands, Nara. My fecking hands."

Before I can say anything to calm him down, he exhales a harsh breath and raises his eyes to mine. "Don't worry. I'm dealing with it. But in answer to your question...no, I won't tell my uncle or anyone else the whole truth."

I understand his hesitancy. After all, he's living in a place full of people whose whole purpose is to support Corvus who hunt and dispatch demons. "Maybe over time you'll feel comfortable sharing with someone there."

He slowly shakes his head like that would never happen. "There was something else etched underneath the message."

My eyebrows shoot up. "What'd it say?"

"E.W."

"Who's that?"

"The watch belonged to my Dad. Evan Wicklow."

I stare at him for a second. "Your dad was a member of the Order?"

A muscle works on his clenched jaw. "Just another thing about him that I didn't know."

"I'm sorry, Drystan." His sarcasm tugs at my heart. "For

what it's worth, there's a lot of stuff I didn't know about my dad until recently either."

"At least he gave you his name."

Resentment rolls off him in such strong waves, all I can do is try to distract him and give him something to focus on. "Maybe the words etched on the watch's back don't mean what you think they mean."

He frowns, skeptical. "There's a reason it was hidden underneath. I can't help but think his message was meant for me. In case I came to the Order."

I smile a little. "If that's true, regardless of its meaning, the fact your father cared enough to leave you a message should make you feel good."

He grunts and glances away, mumbling, "I suppose." Swinging his attention back to me, his eyes flash with renewed resentment. "It also means he kept even more secrets from me...and my mum. It's bad enough he never married her, but neither of us had a clue about his past in England. We only just discovered he had a brother after my father died."

I push my hair over my shoulder and try to think what I would do if I found myself in the middle of the Order's headquarters. "If you want my advice, I think you should take advantage of your time at the sanctuary. Try to find out about the Order's past and your dad's part in it. With your ability to sneak into places, I'll bet you can uncover more. Maybe there's some documentation or records that refer to your dad. I can't believe it hasn't come up that he was part of the Order."

He grimaces. "That's the thing. *No* one has mentioned it at all. Then again, most of the people here are much younger than my uncle and might not remember my dad. My father had been in Wales almost thirty years. But no, my uncle hasn't said anything about his younger brother ever being here."

"Why don't you ask him?"

His mouth slants stubbornly, then a thoughtful look replaces his distrustful one. "Some of the kitchen staff are older. Maybe if I get them talking, they'll reveal something…"

"See, there you go. You have a place to start. And don't forget to look for records too."

He nods, offering a half smile. "I knew you'd have some ideas. Thanks, Nara. I miss you already."

I smile. "You're missed here too."

Movement in my doorway draws my attention. Ethan's leaning on the doorframe, arms crossed. I can't read his shuttered expression. "I've got to go, Drystan. Keep in touch."

He nods and taps the keyboard, logging off.

Once my screen goes dark, Ethan walks into the room. "Your mom sent me up." His focus shifts to my laptop. "I thought he'd be on his way to England by now."

After he pulls a chair up next to mine and sits in it backward, straddling the seat, I answer, "He's already there. That's why he called."

Ethan grunts and folds his arms across the back of the chair.

I ignore his obvious annoyance. "He told me something interesting. His father was a member of the Order at one time."

Ethan shrugs. "I guess that makes sense since his uncle's their leader."

"That's the thing…Drystan's dad never told him about the Order. And his uncle didn't tell him his father had been a member either. Drystan discovered it on his own when he examined the watch his uncle gave him with the Corvus symbol stamped on the back. Apparently the watch was his dad's."

He frowns slightly. "Drystan's going to be a Paladin?"

"I don't know if he will or not. He's having a hard enough time trusting anyone. I can't say that I blame him. His uncle might've been trying to ease him into the idea of becoming a Paladin and joining the Order, but not telling Drystan the truth while he was here in the U.S. around a Corvus was a mistake. I know Mr. Wicklow regrets leaving Drystan unprotected and feels guilt over him being possessed by that demon, but I don't see him forgiving his uncle for that anytime soon. He doesn't trust easily to begin with."

"But he trusts *you*."

My attention drifts to Ethan's clenched hand resting on his forearm. Even though he knows I see Drystan only as a friend, I guess he'll always think of him as a rival. "Well, I'm glad he trusts someone. I think being possessed by that demon affected him far more than he's letting on."

"What makes you say that?"

"Hey guys!" Lainey says, strolling into my room. "Your mom was hanging a wreath on the front door and said you were up here."

More decorations? Sheesh, Mom! Of course only Lainey would manage to look chic in a puffy jacket with a fur-lined hood and bright red Christmas socks. She must've left her designer snow boots by the front door. When she pushes the hood off, revealing her naturally curly red hair, I grin and take the shopping bag from her. "I see you didn't bother with the flat-iron."

"Why bother with this crazy weather." Rolling her eyes, she shrugs out of her jacket, then tosses it onto my bed. "Can you believe they're calling for a full-on blizzard tomorrow night?"

"A blizzard?" I say, holding the bag out for her.

"Yep. That's why I'm here now." She shakes her head and pushes the bag toward me. "Merry Early Christmas."

"Oh, it's for me?"

"I might not get back here for a couple of days if a ton of snow comes, so..." She nods to the bag in my hand. "Open it."

I pull a hot pink T-shirt wrapped in tissue from the bag and hold it up. *Adder's wheel keeper with certified street tread* is printed across the chest in black letters.

Ethan lets out a laugh and hooks an arm over my shoulders. "Love it, Lainey."

She nods, giving him a knowing smile. "Thought you would." Pointing to me, she says, "And you're wearing it the next time we see Ethan play with Weylaid."

"Um...I am?" Blatantly rubbing the fact that Adder's taken in his fans' faces isn't my style. I look at Ethan for some help.

He chuckles and curls his arm, his muscles pulling me close. Pressing a kiss to my cheek, he says, "She'll wear it."

"You'd better." Lainey huffs, putting her hands on her hips. "I don't care if Ethan goes by a stage name, all those girls cat-calling Adder's name need to know who holds the keys to his heart."

When I glance at Ethan, his blue eyes hold mine, full of sincerity. "Yeah, you do."

"If I didn't have Matt, I'd be so jealous of you two right now."

Laughing at Lainey, I reach over and hug her. "Matt's a lucky guy. Thank you for the gift."

Lainey hugs me back, then grabs the bag in my hand with a sigh. "Remind me never to pick you as my Easter egg hunting buddy. You suck at turning over every rock."

"Huh?"

Reaching inside the bag, she pulls out something small wrapped in tissue. "Here's your main gift. The T-shirt was just for fun."

I unwind the tissue and a pair of quarter-sized silver hoop earrings falls into my hand. "Aw, thank you, Lainey."

"Put them on," she says, gesturing to my earring-free ears.

As I slip the earrings on, I smile and nod to the small box on my dresser wrapped in red paper and sporting a small white bow on top. "That's your gift. Open it."

With a wide grin, Lainey retrieves the box and quickly tears through the paper.

I grab the bow from the paper she'd torn off and stick it on top of her head as she pulls the silver charm bracelet out of the box.

"It's gorgeous, Nara!" She quickly hands it to me and holds out her wrist.

As I hook the clasp, she inspects the charms I had the jeweler add to the links. "A horseshoe, a wishbone, a four-leaf clover, rabbit's foot, a cat's eye stone, a hand with crossed-fingers and a locket?" Glancing at me in confusion, she says, "I definitely detect a 'good luck' theme here, but what does the locket do?"

I open it and show her the Corvus engraving the jeweler copied from the one Ethan had placed on my ring. "This symbol is also good luck. Always wear this and it will keep you safe."

Lainey rubs her finger over the engraving, then closes the locket and lifts her brown eyes to mine. "Whew, you have no idea how glad I am to hear that about this symbol."

Ethan and I exchange glances. "It's a pretty rare symbol," I say. "Have you seen it before?"

Lainey bites her lip and nods. "Yeah, Matt's been drawing it a lot lately. He said he keeps seeing it and can't get the image out of his head. At first I thought it was kind of neat, but now I don't know. He can't seem to stop drawing it. It's the same image over and over. Like the one in the locket, but different."

"How is it different?" Ethan asks.

Lainey doesn't see it, but I notice the tension in his face as she says, "Well, it looks like it started out like the one Nara has inside the locket, but the way Matt's drawing it, you realize that the one black bird was never a bird at all but thousands of smaller black birds that had formed the larger shape. It gave me a sense that it's crumbling, or falling apart..." Straightening her shoulders, she offers a shaky smile. "He plans to get it tattooed on his arm, so I'm glad it means good luck."

What does Matt's drawing mean? How is he seeing the Corvus symbol? I clasp Ethan's hand and ask Lainey in a calm voice even though my insides are tense with worry. "His parents are going to let him get it?"

She nods. "Yeah, his dad thought it was cool."

I shake my head and nod toward her bracelet. "Tell him I said to get the tattoo like the one in your charm if he has to get one."

"And for God's sake, tell him to get it where he can cover it up, like on his hip or something."

"Why?" Lainey asks, eyes wide at Ethan's brusque comment.

I squeeze his hand to calm him down. "Depending on the job Matt plans to go into, certain ones won't allow tattoos to be seen. Why limit his options?"

When Lainey cocks an eyebrow, her gaze shifting to the ink on both of Ethan's arms, he raises our clasped hands, a wolfish smile tilting his lips. "I don't plan on having a career that'll keep me from showing mine."

"But it's definitely something Matt should consider," I

jump in. "I hear removing tattoos is more time consuming and costly than getting them."

"Oh crap." Eyes wide, Lainey moves to pick up her coat. "Matt wants to be a doctor. I'd better get going." Shrugging into it, she continues, "He was looking up a friend's name, an artist who does tattoos, when I spoke to him earlier."

"Thank you for my earrings, Lainey," I say as I walk her to my doorway. "If Matt has any questions about the symbol, tell him to call me or Ethan."

"Will do." Lainey nods, then glances at Ethan over my shoulder. "Merry Christmas, you two. See you after the snowpocalypse is over."

Once Lainey leaves, I turn to say to Ethan, "That was interesting," but I bump into him instead. His chest is flush with mine as he cups my jaw. I shake my head and chuckle. "I'll never get used to your speed—"

Ethan kisses me, cutting off my comment. I smile against his mouth and press my hands to his hard chest, kissing him back. His fingers slide along my jaw, just before he deepens our kiss.

My heart pounds and I surrender to the magnetic pull of his mouth moving over mine while his other hand applies pressure against the small of my back, tugging me closer, aligning my hips with his.

Just when our breathing starts to elevate and his hand slides to my rear, Ethan breaks our kiss and presses his forehead to mine. I sigh quietly, loving his intensity so much my heart aches. Touching his cheek, I say, "What was that for?"

He lifts his head, his thumb moving along my jaw in a rhythmic caress. "It just feels like something new is always being thrown at us." Cupping my face in a tender hold, he continues, "But you and I—this—it's the one thing I know is real. It's not sand shifting under our feet. *We're* rock solid."

I feel the tension in his hold even if he doesn't realize it.

Clasping his wrists, I squeeze gently. "I'm here, Ethan. I'm not going anywhere. Yes, there seems to be constant changes and things tugging us in many directions, but I'm not running away."

He kisses my forehead and murmurs, "I refuse to be kept away from you."

Kept away? What is he talking about? I start to ask, but he pulls me close and wraps his arms tight around me like he's afraid I'll disappear.

I lay my head on his chest and hug him back. No one's trying to keep us apart. Why would he think— I quickly lift my head. "Did my mom say something to you about us downstairs?"

He looks down at me, confused. "No, why? Is something going on?"

"I'm just wondering why you're suddenly so worried someone's going to try to keep me from you." I pat his jaw. "No one has the power to do that. Not even my parents."

"Parents?" His brows pull together. "Did your dad say something?"

I start to say no, then realize it's probably best to give him a heads up. "Um, I meant to tell you that while my dad was in my room this morning he used the bathroom and happened to see the wastebasket I hadn't cleaned out yet."

It takes a second for Ethan to make the connection, but when he does, his hold on me tightens. "What did he say?"

I shrug. "He tried to play the parent card. I called him on it and told him he didn't know me well enough to judge me or my choices. Mom knows I'm on the pill; she's the one who asked me about it a while back after she first met you, so..." I trail off and shrug. Ethan doesn't need to know that my conversation with my dad was about his concerns over him being so darkly layered on top of the sexually active part.

Ethan's blue eyes never leave mine. "So what'd he say to that?"

I roll my eyes. "Of course he's not thrilled. He still sees me as a little girl. Anyway, I just thought it would be better to warn you so you're not blind-sided if my dad tries to corner or intimidate you."

Ethan shakes his head. "You're the only one who can intimidate me."

Snickering, I hook my arms around his neck. "Well, I think you're pretty awesome and I have no intention of getting rid of you any time soon."

His eyes widen and he grips my waist. "Any time *soon*?"

I nod. "You know…until things start to get boring —*Ethan*," I shriek, squirming between gasps of laughter as his fingers dig into my sides.

"Boring?" he says, tickling me mercilessly. "I can't imagine that ever happening. But just in case…" He pauses and grasps my waist, lifting me in the air until my eyes are level with his. "I promise you this, Nara Collins. If the Corvus stuff disappeared tomorrow, I love you enough to do whatever it takes to keep it interesting between us. Boring will never be a word you will use to describe what happens in our relationship. That, I can guarantee."

The sensation of his hands touching my skin under my shirt makes me tingle all over, needing more. When my eyes meet his, I feel the want and need, the intense pull of his emotions, just as much as I did earlier today in the backseat of his car.

Sobering, I set my hands on his shoulders, then slide my legs around his trim hips. Ethan doesn't resist a second, he settles me against his body like I'm made to fit there. While I skip my fingers along his skin, then twine them in his hair, his hungry gaze searches my features.

"I love you back just as much," I say. "Nothing about you bores me, even watching you sleep."

A dark eyebrow shoots up, and his hands flex along my hips. "You watched me sleep?"

I nod and run a finger down his nose. "You looked very peaceful."

"That's only because I'd spent the night with you, Sunshine." His lips curl in a smirk when my finger starts to slide past them.

I gasp in surprise when he quickly clamps his teeth around my finger, then closes his lips around it and sucks the tip deeper into his mouth. His intense eyes hold mine as he slides his tongue sensually over and around my skin, soothing away the slight pain he'd inflicted.

"Torturer," I say, breathlessly, my body screaming for so much more.

"Nara," Mom calls from downstairs. "Can you and Ethan come take care of breaking down all these boxes from the Christmas stuff I bought? Trash pickup's in the morning, and I want all this out of the way before guests arrive tomorrow."

"Okay, we'll be right down."

Ethan's eyes spark with heat as I regretfully slide my finger from his mouth. Kissing my knuckle, he says, "My sweet lollypop," then sets me down and rasps in a low, husky voice against my ear, "Never, ever boring."

His seductive promise makes my stomach flutter and my body tingle all the way down the stairs.

CHAPTER 8

NARA

*A*fter we'd taken care of the boxes for Mom, Ethan and I return to my room to look over Freddie's book. As I sit on my bed with the blue book in hand, I raise an eyebrow when Ethan pulls the chair close to my bed and sits on it backward once more. "Come sit over here with me."

He slowly shakes his head. "Not a good idea."

"What? Why?"

He slides his attention from me to the pillows, his lips quirking. "Sitting with you will give me too many ideas that have nothing to do with studying a book."

"Oh." I giggle, my face turning warm. "Um, good point."

Ethan leans over the back of the chair and slowly runs his finger down my cheek, amusement flashing in his eyes. "You're blushing."

I smack his hand away. "Am not."

"It's adorable." He chuckles, his lips twisting wickedly.

My hands shake as I clutch the book. "If you don't stop looking at me like that, we'll never get this done."

He straightens and spreads his hands, eyebrows raised in innocence. "Like what?"

"Like you—"

"Want to devour you?" Resting his muscular arm on the back of the chair once more, his voice lowers to a toe-curling resonance. "I do. Very much, Sunshine."

As my face flames, I laugh at myself. He's so deliciously irresistible, I can't help it. "At least you're honest."

He dips his head, eyeing me. "Always with you."

We exchange a charged look, but when I drop my gaze to open the book in my hands, he says, "So are we going to talk about it, or are we just going to ignore the bomb Lainey dropped on us earlier about Matt?"

"You mean *unknowingly* dropped," I say, my eyes snapping to his.

"Do you think Matt is having some kind of premonition?" he asks.

I shake my head. "I'm not sure, but why else would his mind be filled with the Corvus symbol in the process of exploding? It's not like he just happened to run across it somewhere. I searched many resources, from the web to books, and *I* never found anything close."

Ethan frowns. "Exploding? That's not what Lainey said. She said hundreds of birds are coming off the black raven in the symbol. That could just as well represent every single Corvus out there that has a piece of the Master Corvus inside them." He shrugs. "The image Matt keeps seeing could be the symbolic representation of the Corvus' overall existence."

I pick up the pen from my nightstand and tap it on the book. "Or it could represent something that happened in the past."

Ethan's brow furrows. "What happened in the past?"

"Remember when Mr. Wicklow told me about that day thirty years ago when the Master Corvus killed the Order's leader and decimated the sanctuary?" When he nods, I continue, "Well, the day that happened, Mr. Wicklow said that all the existing Corvus collapsed and the raven spirit left their bodies."

Ethan's brows elevate. "So all the Corvus the Order had found and helped up to that point, suddenly ceased to exist?"

"Yes. Drystan's uncle also said that the Order has been running blind since that day in their quest to find any new Corvus that came into existence after that. I'm pretty sure the Corvus medallion that had always helped the Order locate newly formed Corvus stopped working that day too."

"It could mean that, I suppose." Ethan rubs his hands over his face. "Or it could mean something entirely different."

I sigh and nod. "One thing we know for sure. It means *something*. Why else would Matt keep seeing it?"

"Agreed."

"I think you should try to talk to Matt and see if you can get anything more out of him than what he's told Lainey."

His eyebrows shoot up. "You think he's not telling her everything?"

"This *is* Lainey we're talking about. I'm sure Matt has figured out what I already know about my friend. If she ever finds out that all her friends have some unique ability that we didn't tell her about, I'm pretty sure she'd stop talking to all of us. I half wonder if she knows about mine. She's always fussing at me about keeping things to myself."

Ethan smiles and rests his chin on his arms. "When I realized you had some kind of ability, but I didn't know what it was, I was surprised that Lainey hadn't picked up on it."

"Don't be all that surprised," I say in a dry tone. "I just found out Mom has known about mine and Dad's gift all along."

"Are you serious?" He sits up, expelling a disbelieving laugh. "She knows?"

"Just that we have some kind of intuitiveness, but not exactly what it is. I got really mad at her about the fact she never asked Dad about it...or me for that matter. She says she tried to tell me I was special when I was little, but I didn't want to hear it." Shrugging, I force myself to calm down. "The only good thing that came out of it is that I got her to agree to invite you and Dad to dinner tomorrow night."

"Uh, wait...isn't David coming too?"

I nod, then grimace. "I didn't think that one through so well. I was so focused on the fact Mom wouldn't even acknowledge Dad's presence in the same room. At least she'll have to talk to him some at dinner."

Ethan raises his eyebrows. "Dinner should be interesting."

I shrug. "So now you see why I've come to the conclusion that it's perfectly possible Lainey might know about me, but she doesn't want to acknowledge it. And I'm fine with keeping things status quo. Lainey's life will be far less worrisome if she doesn't know." Shrugging, I glance at the ring on my hand decorated with the same symbols of protection Ethan has on the dragon tattoo on his arm, including the Corvus symbol. "Anyway, since I'm never taking this ring off, I'm just like any ordinary girl with regular dreams now, so there's nothing to tell."

Ethan laughs hard, his blue eyes sparkling. "There's nothing ordinary about you."

I grin and lower my head in a mock bow. "That's a high compliment, oh Master Corvus, sir."

Ethan tenses, his face turning somber. "I'm not the Master Corvus."

I instantly regret saying anything, even teasingly. When I

start to change the subject, Ethan flashes a cocky grin. "But you can call me *Master* all you want, Sunshine."

Rolling my eyes, I pick up my hot pink pillow and hit him with it. "Just make sure you talk to Matt. Now let's get back to Freddie's book.

"What exactly did Fate say about it?"

I close my eyes and try to remember his exact words—words he hadn't wanted to tell me but was bound to do so once I'd answered his question honestly and sincerely. "He said, 'The answers start and end with the raven book. Go back to its creation.'"

"Hmm, starts and ends, huh?" Ethan takes the book and turns it around in his hands, inspecting the unique metal findings that pop open to reveal a hidden compartment behind the bound pages and the book's spine. Well, the findings only open once the triskele necklace my grandmother left for me is aligned with the same Celtic symbol stamped on the book's spine.

"I remember you saying that Madeline was given exact instructions for everything on this book." Ethan glances up at me. "That makes me think that whatever clues we're hoping to find must somehow have something to do with the cover."

"Okay, that makes sense." Taking the book from him, I inspect the front, the spine and then the back, looking for inspiration. Then I do the same on the inside of the cover, running my finger down the area where it adheres to the book. When I flip to the end to do the same with the inside of the back cover, the library's checkout card holder falls out of the book.

Ethan catches it before it hits the floor. His eyebrows lift as he hands it back to me. "I didn't realize this book came from a library in London."

I shrug and tuck the holder back inside the book, planning to glue it back later. "That's where Madeline lives, so it makes sense that's where it must've resided at one time."

"Has anyone checked it out?" he asks, leaning forward to check out the due date stamp.

I tap on the blank card. "Apparently not."

Ethan's eyebrows shoot up. "Since Freddie had this book for more than a couple of decades, can you imagine the astronomical fine if it had been?"

I start to laugh, then something Madeline said hits me. I quickly flip the book to look at the filing code stamped on the spine. "Let's see if it's still in the library's system."

I hand Ethan the book, then move over to my laptop to type in The Library of London.

A few keystrokes later, I glance up from my laptop. "Hmm, it shows there's a book there."

"Why does that surprise you?" He lifts it up. "I'm sure they replaced it once this one went missing."

"That's just it." I nod to the book. "I'm pretty sure that it's supposed to be one of a kind."

"Are you saying there isn't another one out there like this?"

I quickly search the Internet, looking for the title. "Nope. There's not another one listed anywhere else. Tell me the book's ISBN number."

Once Ethan reads it off, I type that in. I shake my head. "There aren't any other books out there. That's the only one."

Ethan frowns. "Then why is it showing that the book is checked in at that library?"

I bite my lip. "I don't know. Maybe they just never updated their system."

"Is it possible that Madeline might've created two books?"

"She wouldn't do that."

"But what if she did?"

"You mean like a backup copy?"

He nods. "She created this one to Michael's specifications, so he has to be the one who put that hidden scroll in this book. If she did make a copy, maybe he put another one in that version too."

Hope fills my heart. I quickly fire off an email to Madeline to confirm his theory. "If it's there, maybe its secret isn't lost."

Ethan holds my gaze with serious eyes. "You're worried you won't remember, aren't you?"

I hate to admit it out loud, so I close my eyes and whisper, "I'm worried I've screwed up. That I won't remember what was on that scroll I found before it disintegrated in my hand."

My eyes flutter open when Ethan's hand touches the back of my head. I never even heard him move; he's so stealthy. He squats next to me and runs his fingers down the blonde strands. "I have every faith you will remember when you need to, but if it gives you peace of mind to consider the possibility there's another book, then yeah, let's go with that theory."

"I've sent an email to Madeline asking if she created another book. If she did and it's there in the library like the system says, then we need to get it." Offering a half smile, I say, "Drystan invited me to London this summer. He wants to show me around the Order's sanctuary. While I'm there I could visit the library and retrieve it then."

"Show you around? More like he's inviting you so his uncle can try to convince you to become a Paladin."

I tilt my head, tensing in frustration. "What do you have against me being a Paladin? Do you think I'd suck at it? That I'm not tough enough?"

Ethan shakes his head. "Why would you think that?

You'd make an awesome Paladin. Their mission might be to help the Corvus, but I just can't bring myself to trust the Order."

"Why? Are you worried I'll fall in love with another equally stubborn Corvus?" I tease.

"Not until you *mentioned* it," he growls, disgruntled, then his scowl morphs into a dark, sensual smile. "No, it's an entirely selfish reason; I want you all to myself, Sunshine."

He's so unrepentant, I can only chuckle. "Well, I doubt you have to worry about Drystan trying to help his uncle recruit me. He hasn't said anything about becoming a Paladin. I told you he doesn't trust anyone right now. Seems you have more in common than you thought."

Ethan frowns at my suggestion. "Here's a better plan. Remember that 'trip through history' coming up next semester that Mr. Hallstead mentioned?"

"Yeah, what about it?"

He gives me a knowing smile. "He's taking the class to London."

"Really?" I smile and grab his arm. "That's perfect! But he said he wasn't announcing what the trip is until we got back from Christmas break. How do you know already?"

"He told me while I stayed after school to go over the stuff I'd missed while I was in the hospital."

"This is going to be great. I can't wait to go with you."

He shakes his head. "I can't go. I want to, but it'll cost almost two grand. I can't make that kind of money in a couple of months."

Tension flows through me. "Maybe Samson can loan you the money?"

Ethan's face sets in stubborn lines. "He could, but I won't ask him to. He bought me my car. That's already above and beyond. I couldn't ask for more from him."

"I understand," I say, my shoulders slumping. I hate that he won't be able to experience London with me.

He folds his hand over mine on his arm. "But at least you'll be with a group, Nara. I'm sure you'll get some breakout time, and you can slip off to the library. Just…keep your eyes open."

I snort. "Yeah, libraries and I don't seem to mix well."

"I want to be there." His fingers tighten on my hand. "You know I do."

I nod and kiss his jaw. "I know. I'll be extra careful."

He frowns. "Promise you'll convince someone to go with you. Just have the person wait around the corner or something while you check to see if the book is there."

"I'll find someone to go with me."

"Good." Ethan stands and kisses the top of my head. "I have to go. Since I'm having dinner here tomorrow night, Samson will probably want to go out to eat tonight."

I raise my eyebrows. "You usually eat out on Christmas Eve?"

He laughs. "Yeah. It's our tradition and one of the few nice meals we splurge on each year."

I quickly stand and grip his hand. "If you'd rather spend tomorrow night with Samson, I understand. I don't want to change your plans."

"No worries. Our parents invited us over to their house earlier in the day tomorrow. I'm sure they'll have food, so he probably won't be hungry for dinner anyway."

I notice the change in his tone and squeeze his hand. "You never know, it might turn out to be a great day with your parents. Give it a chance, okay?"

"It's not like I have a choice." He shrugs, unconvinced. "Samson insisted that we accept their invitation, so—"

My phone rings, cutting him off. Ethan raises an eyebrow

at the "Death of a Shopaholic" ring tone. "Lainey's calling already? She just left."

I click answer and put my phone to my ear. "Hey, Laniey. What's up?"

"You're going to a rave tonight."

I laugh and glance at Ethan. "I am?"

"Yep. It starts at eleven. Matt's in a mood. He has been ever since Drystan left. He needs to blow off some steam, so he and one of his teammates have decided to host a rave in honor of the snow storm about to hit."

When Ethan mouths, "What?" I say, "There's a rave tonight at eleven. Can you go?" Covering the phone, I whisper, "It might be your chance to talk to Matt."

"Make sure Ethan comes," Lainey says loud enough for Ethan to hear.

When Ethan nods, I ask Lainey, "Where are they holding it?"

"In the ElectroMart building."

"Didn't they close that store last year?"

"Yep, it's empty, which makes it the perfect place for a rave. Be sure to park around the side or back. The building has tons of sound proofing due to the stereo equipment they used to sell. Matt's calling it the Snow Rave. Ha! Maybe all the crazed dancing will bring a boatload of snow. Okay, gotta go. Matt's in super plan mode now."

Once I hang up, Ethan pulls me into his arms. "I finally get to take you to a dance."

I snicker and drape my arms over his shoulders. "Yeah, a totally illegal one."

He grins. "You and I have never done the normal way. Why start now?"

CHAPTER 9

NARA

"You'd think people never get out," Ethan says, quietly closing his car door. I shut my side with a quiet click and peer through the flurries coming down at a steady pace, my gaze following the very long line of parked cars that snakes from the side to the back of ElectroMart's two story building.

"Wow, it's so quiet. Lainey wasn't kidding about the solid walls. I can't hear a thing."

When we turn the corner, someone in the shadows up ahead opens ElectroMart's back door. Booming base thrums through the night air before it's quickly swallowed by the metal click of the door closing.

Ethan chuckles and reaches for my hand. "That's some excellent sound proofing."

I left my coat in the car, and even though I'm wearing a silky cream scarf around my neck to cover the gauze, my thin light pink sweater and skinny jeans provide little warmth. Ethan sees me shivering and instantly pulls me close to his toasty warmth. I grip the back of his dark blue Henley and snuggle against his solid frame, inhaling his appealing masculine smell as we make our way to the building.

Two guys bundled in thick parkas, one on either side of the door, stiffen to attention with our approach.

"Password," the taller of the two says in a gruff voice.

I blink at them, then shake my head and laugh. Lainey didn't think to tell me the password. "Um, hi guys. We're here for the snow rave. Lainey invited us."

When Ethan starts to reach for the door handle, the shorter guy in a Russian style hat grabs his forearm and steps between him and the door. "Sorry, but if you don't have the password, we can't let you in."

Tensing beside me, Ethan says in an eerily calm tone, "I'm going to give you one chance to let go of my arm."

I press my hand against Ethan's rock hard stomach to hold him back and quickly say to the taller guy who'd also stepped in front of Ethan. "It's Lochlan."

When both guys nod and let us enter, Ethan slides a surprised look my way and calls over the music filtering through the heavy door at the end of the hallway. "How'd you know the password?"

I chuckle as we stop just outside the door. "It's Lainey's dog's name. She has used it before."

Ethan snorts. "Does anyone pay attention to security tips? 'Never use your pet's name' is like Password one-oh-one."

I reach for the doorknob. "Lainey's dad is a cop, remember? She uses it for things like the locker combination at the indoor pool, not to protect her computer or bank account info." Smiling up at him, I turn the handle. "I can't wait to see you dance to rave music."

A wicked grin quickly replaces his serious expression. Clasping my free hand, he steps close and whispers in my ear, "Darkness and adrenaline are my specialty. Get ready for me to rock your world in the middle of mayhem."

While a shudder of excitement slides across my skin, Ethan doesn't give me a chance to comment as he folds his hand over mine and we turn the knob together.

The second we step inside the big room, colorful, flickering stobe lights engulf us. Black lights' purple hue beams down from the ceiling as we're showered with a spray of glitter. Two girls standing on either side of us grab up new handfuls of glitter from table-top buckets and shout over the heavy drum beats and synthesized sound, "Now you'll sparkle like the snow. Get your drunk on and dance 'til you drop!"

While Axwell's "In My Mind" blares from the speakers, Ethan and I glance at each other. We're sparkling all over, the black light effect setting off the glitter. I pour a beer from the keg, but Ethan shakes his head when I offer him one. Squeezing my fingers, he tugs me into the crowded space full of a couple hundred people drinking and dancing frenetically to the up-tempo song.

As we dance to the music, I drink my beer and scan the crowd for Lainey. I'm just finishing my drink when my attention snags on my best friend standing on the raised stage in the far corner of the room. She's next to Matt, whose blond head is bent close to talk to the DJ. Just when Matt straightens and grins, circling his finger in the air, a new song starts to play and "Wake Me Up" by Avicii pumps out of the speakers.

The beer is already going to my head, and mixed with the crowd going wild over the familiar song, amps my excitement while we match our dancing to the slower, opening rhythm. Just when the song speeds up during the first fast-paced chorus, Matt jumps off the stage and then grips Lainey by the waist, twirling her into the crowd to enjoy the music.

"I see Lainey and Matt," I say to Ethan. "Let's make our way over to them."

Once I throw away the cup, Ethan helps me shoulder my way through the crush of people. As soon as Lainey sees me, she squeals and hugs me tight, yelling in my ear, "Isn't this the best party ever? I think it rivals the Winter dance."

Matt hasn't even noticed us. His eyes are closed and he's jumping and waving a beer cup in the air, totally lost in the music.

While Ethan taps Matt on the shoulder and speaks to him, I say to Lainey. "You weren't kidding about Matt blowing off steam. He's really into this, isn't he?"

"I need another beer just to cool off." Lainey pushes her sweaty red hair off her face. Fanning herself, she glances at Matt who's still dancing as he speaks to Ethan. "Yeah, he's definitely been edgier than usual lately. I think tonight will really be good for him."

I take in her white tank top and Matt's bare chest glistening with sweat and glitter and snicker. "I see you're both dressed for snow weather."

She laughs and waves her hand toward the stage. "My snow boots and sweater are back there. Matt stripped them off me the moment I walked in, and whew, I'm glad he did. It's burning up in here with all this body heat. I'd tell you to strip down to your tank too, but I see you're not wearing one. Nice bra, by the way."

"Huh?" I glance down at myself and gulp. The black light is making my white lace bra glow like my sweater is made of a sheer material. Ethan and I had been in the crush of people earlier, but now that there's a couple feet of space, everything's on display. I might as well be shirtless.

Just when I start to fold my arms across my chest, Lainey

grabs my wrists and pulls them to my side, shaking her head. "Oh, no you don't. You look hot, Nara. Let your inner sex goddess free tonight and...um, wow. I think Ethan's just noticed too." Leaning close she says in my ear, "What he can convey with just one look is panty melting. If I didn't love Matt..."

Before I can even respond to her comment, she grabs Matt's hand and says, "We'll be back after the steam has cleared."

Matt looks around, confused. "Steam? But you said we didn't need the dry ice machines."

Ethan's fingers fold around my elbow once Lainey pulls Matt into the crowd, his deep voice resonating in my ear. "Half the guys around us have noticed the effect the black light's having on your sweater."

I can't tell by his tone if he's upset, turned on, or somewhere in between. Should I embrace my inner sex goddess like Lainey suggested? I start to say something when a couple of dark-haired guys walk up, and the taller of the two hands me a beer. "Hey, gorgeous. I see your hand's empty. Have a beer."

Just as I smile and hand the cup back, saying, "No thanks," Ethan slides his hand from my elbow to my free hand and narrows his eyes on the guy. "Before you give that to the next girl, it had better not have anything in it other than beer."

I've heard stories of guys slipping drugs in drinks at parties, so I appreciate Ethan trying to look out for others. His hard stare is fierce, making me glad I've never been the recipient of that side of his intensity. Even in the semi-darkness, I can see the guy's face go pale. He stiffens and quickly shakes his head. "It's just beer, man."

Once the guy and his friend blend back into the crowd, I

peek down at my sweater then meet Ethan's steady gaze, grimacing. "Who knew, right?"

Alesso's remix of One Republic's "If I Lose Myself" starts up, and while the sensual trance-like words fill the room, Ethan slides his hand across my belly, then cups my hip and slowly turns me to face him. "Ready to have your world rocked?"

Heart ramping, I grip his shoulders and my pulse thrums as we begin to dance to the music, our hips moving in perfect sync. "Look at me," he says, his voice entrancing, his heavy gaze on me beyond charismatic. It's near hypnotic.

When I meet his dark eyes, everything seems to slow, the music and sensation of people crushing around us fades until all I hear and feel is the music's muffled rhythmic bass thumping against my chest. "It's just you and me now, Sunshine. Listen. What do you hear?"

Layered on top of the bass is a steady upbeat *thump, thump* sound. It repeats again and again. I curl my fingers around his neck, awe filling me. "It's a heartbeat."

A slight shake of his head. He pulls my hips flush against his and I settle my hands around his waist. "It's our hearts beating."

I blink several times. "Together? At the same time? That's impossible."

He lifts a dark eyebrow and moves his hands from my hips to my upper back. While we slowly move to the seductive music, he pulls my chest against his. The second we connect, I tingle everywhere, but I also feel what my ears hear: our hearts pounding in the same slow, steady rhythm.

"But how?"

Ethan folds a hand on the back of my neck, his thumb tracing my jawline. Bending close, he feathers a kiss along my temple, then whispers huskily in my ear, "Magic."

When he kisses my cheekbone, then my jaw, I guide my

fingers under his shirt and grip him close. I don't want to pull away, to disconnect our tethered hearts. I hadn't imagined the syncing that happens between us when we're close like this. The feeling is beyond surreal. It's bone deep and exactly as he described: magical.

The second his mouth covers mine in a soul-wrenching kiss, the heartbeat starts to speed up and my chest feels like it's expanding. I gasp and press my mouth harder against his.

Ethan's hand slides into my hair at the same time his tongue teasingly touches mine. "You totally shred me, Nara," he murmurs against my mouth, then cups the back of my head and grips my hair, deepening our kiss.

I kiss him with equal intensity, my fingers fisting in his shirt. His hands move to my back, grasping me tight. He enthralls me, engaging all my senses. I lose myself in his arms, shutting out everything but this moment of pure bliss. The sudden sound of piercing whistles yanks me out of the spell he's woven around us.

A crowd close to us has stopped dancing and is whistling and cheering. Several people are openly staring at my hands where I'd unconsciously pulled Ethan's shirt halfway up his back.

Embarrassed, I quickly yank his shirt down and start to step back, but he wraps his arms around my waist, locking me in place, an arrogant grin on his face.

"Ethan!" I say in a quiet hiss.

Pressing a chaste kiss to my forehead, he murmurs for just my ears, "Let them cheer. We're awesome together."

As the crowd resumes their crazed dancing, I laugh despite myself. "You definitely rocked my world."

Ethan lets out a bark of laughter, then grabs my hand and spins me in a circle. "The feeling's definitely mutual, Sunshine."

We dance with Lainey and Matt for another hour. During that time, Ethan tried to talk to Matt. The first time, Matt was too busy dancing. The second time he tried, Matt slowed down his dancing to listen, but then he just shook his head and pointed to his ear, "Sorry, dude. It's too loud. Can't hear you." Matt was just too hyped up for any conversation that didn't involve whoops, screams and yelling for "more house sound."

Wiping a sheen of sweat from my brow, I glance at my watch, then tap Lainey on the shoulder. "I need to be home before one. Mom gave me several errands to do tomorrow." Hugging her tight, I say, "Merry Christmas. This was an awesome rave. I think you should be our party organizer from now on."

Lainey snorts. "Can't you just see it now...my future career as a party planner?"

I tilt my head and smile. "That's actually not a bad idea. According to the listings I saw on career day, if you're really good, the salary can get pretty high."

"Paid to party. I like it," Lainey says, then sighs dramatically and waves me on. "Go if you must. The snowpocalypse will soon be here, giving me my very first white Christmas." Raising her cup of beer, she cheers loudly, "Here's hoping we'll dance ourselves into five feet of snow."

The crowd around us joins in Lainey's chant, and fifteen seconds later the whole room is chanting and swaying in a wave that ripples across the entire space.

Yep, Lainey's got what it takes to make any place rock. Smiling, I wave goodbye.

It's still and quiet outside once the building's door shuts behind us. Even the two guys who were guarding the door earlier must've finally gone inside to party. I sigh happily as light snow continues to fall.

While we walk along the line of parked cars, Ethan

wraps his arm around my waist and pulls me close. "What are you thinking?"

I put my hand out. The moment the snow hits my dance-warmed skin, it instantly melts. "I love how peaceful snow is. Even when it comes down heavy and fast, it's quiet. Rain can be so loud. Some might find the sound of pounding rain soothing, but to me...snow is peaceful and tranquil."

Ethan smirks. "Heavy rain is much easier to maneuver in. A blizzard can be completely incapacitating. You can swim through waist high flooding, but you can't easily wade through four feet of snow."

"Uh. Thanks for bursting my rose-colored bubble."

Ethan chuckles and glances down at me. "I was just playing devil's advocate. Snow does have one attribute that rain doesn't though. Something that makes it definitely worth your admiration."

"Oh, really? I'd love to hear it."

We turn the corner of the building, and Ethan stiffens. His shoulders tense, his hand pulls me to a stop. Tugging me behind him, he says. "Get back inside the building."

His tone is dangerously low. I peer around his shoulder to see a guy in a brown leather jacket leaning casually against Ethan's car, boots crossed at his ankles, and his hands shoved in jean pockets.

The college-aged, sandy-haired guy gives me a leering smile before he shifts his line of sight to Ethan. "I would warn you...that next time...don't let your girl reveal your sword in public." He shrugs and pushes off the car. "But that'd be kind of pointless since you'll soon be dead, *Corvus*."

Oh, God. I brought this on Ethan. I hadn't meant to expose his tattoo. I guess if you know what to look for, even half the blade is enough to alert a demon, but why didn't Ethan sense the demon in the rave?

Ethan's gaze never leaves the demon while he pushes me away from him and grates out, "*Go*, Nara."

I turn and run back the way we came, guilt knotting my stomach. A couple inches of snow has fallen since we entered the rave. My feet slip on the powdery surface, making it hard to run with confidence. I slow my pace to keep from face-planting, glancing back once to see Ethan hitting the demon with such force, the guy tumbles over the row of cars, landing along the edge of trees that line the side of the building. I want to stay and try to help Ethan, but I don't want to be the reason he's distracted from the battle.

While Ethan veers around the car after the demon, I reach the corner of the building and slam into a tall, barrel-chested guy with slick black hair. I saw him dancing in the rave earlier. Before he can get a good look at what's going on behind me, I grip his jacket and say, "We need to go back inside. It's not safe out here right now."

Instead of looking worried, he clasps my arms and nods toward the sound of fists connecting with bone, bloodlust in his eyes.

Ice fills my veins when the guy tracks Ethan and the demon's movements, a half-crazed smile tilting his lips. "We're staying right here. I have a feeling this battle's going to be worth the phone call I made to that demon."

"You called him?" I rasp in disbelief.

He quickly turns me in his arms and bends close to my ear, sheer admiration in his voice. "You have to admit the power they possess is awe-inspiring."

Ethan glances our way and fury enters his dark eyes.

I call out a warning too late.

The demon slams his fist into Ethan's stomach and then kicks him in the chest, sending him flying against the building's cinderblock wall.

"Ethan!" I scream at the same time I stomp on the rat-bastard's foot.

When he involuntarily bends from the pain, I throw my elbow back and jab him in the nose.

I don't feel an ounce of guilt when I hear a crunch and see blood spurt onto the snow at our feet.

I jerk away and run toward Ethan who's crumpled on the ground by the building, unmoving.

I only get a few feet away when I'm quickly yanked back, blinding pain radiating at the base of my skull. The bastard has grabbed a handful of my hair. Turning his fist, he clutches more strands and tugs until I cry out in pain.

Holding his other hand under his bloody nostrils, he bites out, "You fucking broke my nose, bitch. I'm going to beat you until you beg me to kill you once we take care of your boyfriend."

"Let me go or a broken nose will be the least of your worries," I say in a deadly voice I've never used on anyone before.

The demon's leaning over Ethan now. Nudging him with the toe of his boot, he laughs. I ignore the pain in my head and focus all my energy on Ethan. "Wake up, Ethan!"

Just as the demon swings his booted foot toward Ethan's head, Ethan moves with lightning speed. Yanking the demon's foot at the same time he jerks upright, Ethan punches him in the groin.

The hit only momentarily stuns the demon, but it's enough for Ethan to jump to his feet and grab hold of the guy's curly hair. Holding his sword against the demon's throat, he growls, "Enjoy your time in Under."

"Not yet." The demon laughs right before Ethan plunges his sword into his body.

I blink in surprise when I don't see the familiar fog-like

smoke explode from him like it always does when Ethan expels a demon from a human.

"I like this point of view much better," the guy holding me purrs in my ear, the pleased satisfaction in his voice sending chill bumps of fear trickling through me. Before I can turn and try to push the demon out, he grabs either side of my head in a vice hold. "I'm over here, Corvus," he taunts Ethan. "Too bad you're too late to keep me from snapping her pretty little neck."

I scream at the beginnings of a sharp tug on my head, but suddenly Ethan's right in front of me, his sword's handle a mere inch from my cheekbone. Unmoving, I pant frantically. In my periphery, I see the blade jammed into the guy's eye socket.

Vibrating with fury, dark eyes full of cold retribution, Ethan doesn't even blink; he twists the sword and obliterates the guy behind me.

As soon as I'm free, my legs feel boneless, but I can't move, can't collapse. I'm frozen in shock. Ethan tilts his head and slides his hand along my jaw, cupping my cheek in a reverent hold.

We stand there like that for what seems like a full minute, the snow quietly falling down on us, before Ethan blinks and jerks his hand away forcefully, taking a step back.

I'm confused by his action. The thought of him pulling away for any reason brings tears to the surface. They roll down my cheeks, and I hold a hand out to him, my voice shaking. "Ethan?"

He exhales a harsh breath and quickly steps into me, wrapping his arms around me in a fierce hug. "I thought I'd lost you," he says against my hair, his tone wrecked, his hold on me cinching even tighter.

"I'm here. You saved me," I whisper, melting into his

solid strength. "I had no idea demons could jump bodies so quickly."

Ethan tucks his hand under my snow-coated hair, clasping the back of my neck. "A person has to be not only primed to accept the demon, but close at hand. That kind of situation rarely happens."

"I guess the guy from the rave qualified." I sigh against his chest. "He's the one who called the demon after seeing the lower part of your sword tattoo. I'm sorry for exposing you like that."

Ethan shakes his head and tilts my face up so I have to meet his gaze. "Never apologize for loving me, Nara. I can't always hide my back. I try but sometimes people see it. Fortunately, the vast majority have no idea what my tattoo is."

I curl my lips in a wry half-smile. "Guess we weren't so lucky tonight."

Ethan flashes a cocky smile, tension easing out of him. "Hey, we're still breathing, and one more demon is now in Under. I'd call that pretty damn lucky."

"Luck had nothing to do with it. Fast reflexes did. I didn't even see you move. You were just suddenly there."

Ethan drops a kiss on my nose. "I'll always be there, Sunshine. But I think it's important to continue the defense lessons Drystan started with you. After the holidays, that's first on the agenda."

"Are you going to make me get up at the crack of dawn on Saturdays too?"

He gives me a firm look. "Be prepared to work hard. Demons don't hesitate."

"I know I need it, but *ugh*."

He clasps my hand, his expression determined. "It's happening. Come on. Let's get out of here."

Just when we reach his car, a snowflake lands on the tip

of my nose, making me snicker. "Oh yeah, you were going to tell me your opinion on snow."

His fingers fold tighter around mine before he releases my hand to open my car door. "I will, but I'm saving it for later."

"Later, huh?" I raise my eyebrow. "How much later?"

He shakes his head, amused by my persistence. "I'll tell you tomorrow."

CHAPTER 10

NARA

*T*he first thing I do when my eyes pop open the next morning is check my laptop for an email from Madeline. I'm surprised to see that the email I sent her bounced. I send another one, then type in her website address in the Internet browser to see if I'd somehow messed up when adding her email to my address book.

When I get a missing page link instead, I frown and try again. This time I get a "this website no longer exists" error. Frustrated, I backtrack and look up all Madeline Strauss names in the London area. Before, where there were seven names, now there are six. Worry seizes my chest and I widen my search.

Breathing in short, choppy breaths, I scan through London's newspaper obituaries since I last talked to Madeline, then blow out a sigh of relief that I didn't find her name in any death notices or memorial listings.

Though I'm glad nothing bad appears to have happened to her, I tap my desktop pen in frustration that I can't seem to find her either. It's like she never existed.

Rubbing my temples, I close my eyes and try to think of

another way I might contact her, but my mind's blank. I've exhausted all possible ways I know to track a person down.

You'd probably think this place is a grunge-punk scene, Nara, but I saw the perfect spot for a slackline in a park near here.

I sit bolt upright. There is no way I'm making full-on Drystan sentences up in my head now.

Heart racing, I switch over to the video chat program on my laptop. While I scroll to Drystan's user name, another thought hits me. He can help me with the raven book. I try to ping Drystan's account, but it just shows he's offline. I quickly type a note in the private message window, then hit send.

N: Call me as soon as you can. Need your help with something.

I flip back to my inbox and sigh. My email to Madeline bounced again. Five minutes later, an incoming video ping sounds. I quickly click the answer button and Drystan's face pops up.

"Hey, Nara! Talk while I make my way up this embankment." Curved, graffiti-covered bricks and cement disappear behind him. I can see he's wearing my scarf partially tucked into his leather jacket as forest suddenly replaces the blue sky above his head.

Once he reaches the top of the incline and rights the video screen in front of him, I tease, "I see you're putting my scarf to good use."

"It's cold out here," he says, then laughs, eyeing me. "Nice bedhead. So that's what you look like in the morning."

I stick out my tongue, hating how messy, finger-combed hair looks good on him, while I'm sure mine resembles a rat's nest. "I was on a mission this morning. Haven't had a shower yet."

"So what did you need my help with?"

"Remember that raven book that you helped me steal back from the demon who killed Freddie for it?"

He nods. "That's the same book the other demon who possessed me wanted, right? By the way, he really did believe the book held the key to destroying the Master Corvus."

I swallow at the thought of any demon getting ahold of that book. "Yeah, that's the one."

"Why are you asking me about it? He never did find it before he left my body."

"I know. It's safe for now," I say, running my hand through my tangled hair. "While Ethan and I were trying to uncover more about the book, we discovered there's supposedly another copy of the same book in The Library of London. We want to confirm if that is or isn't the case, because I was under the assumption that the book was one of a kind."

He frowns. "What publisher only produces one book?"

He doesn't know about Madeline's involvement in creating the raven book or about the scroll I found inside, so I keep her out of the conversation. "I just know the book was specially created. Since you know what it looks like, would you be willing to go to the library for me and see if another copy of that book really exists?"

"Sure. It'll give me a reason to explore the city more."

"Thank you for doing that. So did you learn anything more about your Dad from the kitchen staff?"

"Some." He sits down and leans back against a tree. "According to them, my father wasn't officially a Paladin, but he was an honorary one."

"What does that mean?"

He picks up a dead leaf, twirling it. "I have no idea. He wasn't assigned a Corvus, but he was a well-respected member of the Order, and a happy-go-lucky guy everyone liked."

I smile at his his use of "guy". He had picked up a few of

our terms during his short stay in the US. "That's a good thing, right?"

He shrugs. "Maggie—she's the head cook—said that he changed after the incident with the Master Corvus. Turned somber and kept to himself. That stoic man is the only father I've ever known. To be honest, I'm not even sure why my dad was here. He didn't have any abilities."

"Maybe he was there because of his brother. Did you ask your uncle about your dad yet?"

He shakes his head. "No. My dad left the sanctuary a few weeks after everything fell apart and never returned."

"I think you should talk to your uncle, Drystan. He's probably the only one who can answer your questions."

"He still hasn't said anything about my father ever being here, Nara. That really pisses me off. Why hasn't he told me?"

"Why don't you tell him you know and see what he says?"

Drystan gives me a doubtful look. At least he doesn't outright refuse my suggestion this time.

"Have you met anyone else there?"

Drystan slides the scarf off and rubs the back of his neck. "I haven't run across any Corvus yet—I get the feeling the Paladins mostly go to them—but I've gotten to know a couple of Paladins here, a guy and girl who are only a couple years older than me. They've been cool to hang with." His eyes light up a little. "Hey, did you know that powers can evolve? I had no clue that was possible."

The incident with David's demon in my kitchen instantly comes to mind, but I'm still not sure what happened, so there's no point discussing it. "What do you mean?"

"The guy, Phillip, could warm things with just his touch, but now he can heat something up until it reaches boiling point or catches on fire. Chloe has acute hearing. She used to be able to hear in the same range as a dog, now she can hear you whisper a building away. It's like that place—the sanctuary—has enhanced their abilities or something."

"Why do you think the sanctuary had anything to do with it?"

"Because both Phillip and Chloe arrived a week ago and they weren't like this until recently."

"What about the other Paladins? Have their powers changed? Have yours?"

"I don't know any of the other Paladins well enough to ask them, but no my abilities are still the same. Maybe I have to be a Paladin for that to happen."

"Are you considering joining the Order now?"

"No."

"Maybe one day—"

"No," he cuts me off, his jaw muscle tensing. "I don't belong there."

"Actually, you might," I say, worried how angry and lonely he seems. I'm glad he's made a couple friends, but I still feel he's holding so much back. I really wish he had someone there he trusted to talk over what he went through being possessed by that demon.

"What's that supposed to mean?" he asks, brows pulled down.

He sounds so accusatory, I laugh. "You're near a park, aren't you?"

"Yeah, how can you tell?" He glances around. "I'm surrounded by woods."

"And you found the perfect place for a slackline, right?"

He sits upright, green eyes widening. "How'd you know that?"

I grin. "You think I'd call the place grunge-punk."

"How..." He swallows and pales. "Are you in my head, Nara?"

"No, I heard you."

"How is that even possible?"

I shrug, unsure. "Maybe being there is enhancing your abilities too. Today was the first time I heard more than my name."

Drystan glances up at the trees and laughs, then his eyes shift to me. "I can't believe this is happening, but it's kind of nice to know you're here with me, at least in my head."

"I'm not in your head, Drystan. It seems to only happen if you think of something where I'm part of the thought. That's when I hear you."

"Still, it's pretty awesome."

I smile, hoping it helps him feel less alone. "I'm always just a ping away."

"Or a thought." He grins, a slight glimmer of the Drystan I knew shining just under the surface.

Laughing, I nod. "Well, now you have something else to explore…maybe the other Paladins you've become friends with can help you test your abilities."

"Possibly." He glances at his watch. "Guess I'd better go if I'm going to find the library. I'll ping,…er, *think* you later."

"Har, har." I snicker, then log off.

CHAPTER 11

ETHAN

*N*o amount of mental gymnastics you do will push me out of your head. I'm a part of you. Get used to it.

I ignore the Corvus' comment and try to focus on something to help me concentrate, but the trees and houses are whizzing past the window so fast there's nothing to focus on. While Samson changes the radio station in his car, I close my eyes and breathe in and out slowly, trying to find an inner focus.

How about we come to an agreement?

I tense, unsure where the spirit is going with this. *Unless it's about you leaving me the hell alone, I'm not interested.*

I promise to no longer take over and put Nara in what you perceive as danger. Not that I'm agreeing that she was ever in danger in the first place—I am Corvus, after all—but you seem unconvinced.

His arrogance really pisses me off. *Your idea of danger and mine do not even come close, Corvus.*

Be that as it may, are you willing to come to an agreement?

I clench my fist on my thigh. So far none of the mental exercises I've read about in the books I bought have worked.

The Corvus seems to delight in my efforts to block him. He chanted during one effort, made annoying raven *tok, tok* sounds during another, and even started singing some strange archaic sounding song during the last.

He was quieter when I wasn't actively trying to block him. Now he won't shut up, but his promise to no longer put Nara in danger definitely gets my full attention. Thank God he doesn't have access to *all* parts of my mind or any negotiation would be fruitless. Nara is my pressure point and he knows it. *What are your terms?*

Let me have control when demons are around.

My suspicion creeps in. *What exactly does that mean?*

I take over your body during battles.

I'm pretty sure I blacked out for a second last night; I was so hyper-focused on saving Nara. That demon jumping bodies like he did...he could've easily taken her from me. The next thing I knew I was cupping her face and the demon was gone. The idea of letting the spirit take control makes me grit my teeth. He's so powerful, I don't want to give an inch. Before I can say anything, he continues, *You said you wanted to know everything that I know. I fight them. You learn. Simple.*

Nothing is simple with this being. Nothing. But Nara's safety is most important to me. What if I had been a split second behind? That's all it would've taken to lose her. *Here's how this will go, Corvus. You can take control* only *if there is no other humans around. No witnesses. No one else will get hurt.*

I agree to your conditions.

He sounds entirely too smug. I tense and start to withdraw my agreement when my brother's voice snags my attention.

"Ethan!"

I glance his way. "What?"

"I had to call your name three times. Where did you go?"

When I don't respond right away, he sighs and gestures to the house in front of us. "We're here."

"Looks like they've downgraded a bit," I say, sweeping my eyes over the modest ranch house. It's probably one-forth the size of our house in Michigan.

"Ethan…" Samson starts to say, then shakes his head. "I need you to try with Dad tonight, okay?"

"*You* walked out on dinner the last time." When all I get is a hard stare, I snort as he pulls the keys from the ignition. "I'm here, aren't I?"

"And none of *that*," he says in a curt tone, keys jingling while he points at me.

"None of what?"

Sighing, he gets out.

I exhale a calming breath and follow my brother to the front door. For him, I'll keep my mouth shut and make the effort.

In ten minutes, I've piled my plate with cold cuts and slices of cheese while I watch with detached amusement as my mom pats her blonde French twist and tries to surreptitiously look around for my dad to rescue her from some older man in a tweed jacket. *If he's so boring, why'd you invite him in the first place, Mom?*

The plate disappearing from my hand quickly grabs my attention. "Hey. Why'd you—"

"Come on. We're leaving," Samson grumbles in my ear before he walks in the direction of the door.

"I'm out of here—" My brother hisses in a low tone once I finally catch up to his fast stride as he shoulders his way through the crowd.

"Calm down, Samson," I whisper and quickly follow him out of our parents' house. "They have a nice spread of food. What would it hurt to stay and eat?" I can't believe I'm being the voice of reason. Nara must've really gotten to me yesterday.

"This is bullshit and you know it, Ethan," he snaps, not even looking at me while we approach his car.

"*Samson, Ethan,*" my father's booming voice calls after us from the porch. "Where are you going? You just got here."

My brother looks up from unlocking his car door, his blond eyebrows pulled together in obvious irritation. "I thought this was a family thing. That you were set on trying to make it work between us. Instead, it's Michigan all over again. Enjoy your holiday party."

When my father's deep blue eyes shift to me, seeking support, I just shrug and open the passenger door. He should know better. There's no changing Samson's mind at this point. It takes a lot to rile my brother, but once his angry meter goes off, budging him is impossible. Why would my dad expect that the stubborn part of his DNA wouldn't come out in his sons?

As we drive away, Samson's car fishtailing in the layer of snow on the road, he hits his dashboard with his palm. "Fuck it!"

I'm shocked to see my brother so upset. I had no idea he truly hoped our parents had changed their ways just because they rented a house here in Blue Ridge for a while.

"I'm still hungry," I say, which works to derail Samson's foul mood.

"You would be." He snorts and rolls his eyes. "I swear, you're eating more than twice as much as you used to. Do you have a camel's stomach?"

Laughing, I punch his shoulder. "You don't remember eating enough for two men when you were seventeen? Dad complained about the grocery bill back then too."

"I can't eat like that now and still stay fit," Samson says, patting his flat stomach.

"Sure you can. Twenty-three year olds just have to work out more," I say, flashing a smartass smile.

"Bite me," he retorts, then turns onto the highway.

"Where are we going?"

Relaxing his tense shoulders, Samson rests his wrist across the steering wheel. "You said you're hungry. We're going to the downtown mall to eat."

And just like that, he brushes aside what occurred like it never happened. Not that I wasn't just as pissed to walk into our parents' home full of fifty or so strangers milling around and chatting about inane things while holding plates of food and glasses of wine. The difference was, I wasn't surprised we were invited to what turned out to be a social neighborhood party. But the moment we walked in the door, Samson stiffened and his face went red all the way up to his blond hair. When his features settled, I thought he'd gotten control over his anger. Clearly, he had much higher hopes than me.

I've never been one to discuss deep feelings with my brother. Yeah, I'm curious why he got so upset, but I figure he'll tell me when he's ready and settle into the seat, secure in the knowledge we'll be eating soon.

As I stroll beside Samson along the brickyard mall, kicking up the snow with my black combat boots, he eyes me while he zips his leather bomber jacket closed. "How can you just wear that thin army jacket? It's freezing out today."

I dig my hands into my jeans' pockets. "I'm good. So, where do you want to grab a bite?"

He nods toward McCormicks. "I haven't been there in a long time. A beer sounds good to me right now."

Of all places for him to pick. I slow my pace. "You...ah, want to eat at a bar?"

He shrugs. "Why not? Their food isn't bad." And without another word, he turns and heads straight for the door.

I follow, hoping to redirect him elsewhere. "How about that Asian fusion place a bit farther down?"

"Nah, this will be good." He reaches for the door handle and pulls. "I heard a house band plays sometimes. If they're here tonight, maybe we'll just eat and hang for a few hours, enjoying the music. That should sound like heaven to you."

Tension flows through me, stiffening my spine, but then I realize it's Christmas Eve. I'm sure the band is off visiting their families and such.

Several college guys are hanging out close to the empty stage, and a few other groups of girls and guys are scattered among the tables. I'm a little surprised at the older couple having a meal near the picture window, but the laidback scene and dark, empty stage instantly relaxes the tension in my body. It's weird to be here during the day, but also quiet, more subdued, which seems to fit my brother's mood. I can tell he's thinking about what just happened even if he's not talking about it.

I order a burger and fries and Samson orders the same. Thankfully the bartender doesn't acknowledge me other than a slight nod before he sets down the food and walks away.

While my brother is busy loading ketchup on his burger, I pull a slim black felt pouch out of my pocket and set in on the table next to his silverware.

His blond eyebrows elevate, and he sets his burger down to wipe his fingers on his napkin. "What's that?"

"Your Christmas present," I say, before taking a bite of my burger.

"I thought we were exchanging tomorrow morning. Your present is under the tree."

I shake my head. "Stop being so traditional and just open it."

He eyes me for a second, then picks up the pouch and

pulls out a black leather watch. "This is a nice gift, Ethan. Thank you."

I can see the question in his eyes. *How can he afford this?* I told him I have a job where I make a bit of under-the-table cash, but he doesn't know about my music. And since Nara wasn't super thrilled I hadn't told her about playing with the band until recently, I doubt he'd be too happy that I hadn't shared it with him either. Staying quiet is for the best. I know my brother and he won't dare ask about my job. Some things we just take on trust.

My stomach tenses when he flips the watch around and runs his thumb over the Corvus symbol on the metal back. I pop a French fry in my mouth and give a sheepish half smile. "I had some of my art added to the back."

I drew the raven yin-yang symbol myself and then had the engraver add it to the back, but it's the message I had engraved in a semi-circle underneath the symbol that my brother's thumb slides over several times. *Brother/Mentor/Role Model/Friend. Thank you for being my whole family.*

He swallows a couple times before he looks up from the watch. "Thanks, little brother. That means a lot."

His voice is gruff, like he's trying not to get choked up. I thanked my brother when he first brought me to Virginia to live with him, but since then I hadn't told Samson how much I appreciate everything he's done for me. After seeing his reaction tonight at our parents' house, it hits me just how much family means to *him,* and I'm really glad I put my full appreciation on the watch. I cough to cover up my own emotional response, then nod toward the gift. "Put it on. You should wear something nicer than that crappy sports watch anyway."

Samson just straps on the watch when someone calls out, "Adder! Awesome. Glad you're here."

I quickly glance up to see Ivan leaning his bald head out

the side door next to the stage. He arches a pierced eyebrow and waves me over. "Get over here and help us with this stuff."

"Why did he call you Adder?" I can feel my brother's surprised gaze on me when I stand. "Is that your job? You handle the equipment for the house band?"

"Adder's just what they call me." I shrug. "And yeah, part of what I do is handling the equipment from time to time. I'll be right back."

"You're going to work? Now?"

I shrug. "How do you think I paid for that watch?" When he involuntarily glances down at my gift, I finish, "Order a beer and relax. I won't be long."

As I walk away, I scroll through my phone, looking for a number I'd stored there. Once I find it, I send a text, then open the door and head toward the back to find out what Ivan needs help with.

After I help Ivan set up his drums—he'd taken the set on a trip earlier in the week—then helped set up cables, amps and other equipment for the guys, I realize a half hour has passed. Finally, I hop off the stage, leaving Ivan and the other band members: Dom, Chance, and Duke discussing their set for the evening and join Samson at the table once more.

My brother is quiet for the next half hour, but when the band starts to warm up, playing a pre-set song, the side of my face starts burning with Samson's intense stare. "What?" I finally say, pulling my focus away from the guys having a last minute discussion over including a new song in the evening's list.

"Well?" Samson spins his hand. "I'm going to skip over the part that you're underage and assume a fake ID got you access, and ask the more pertinent question. When were you going to tell me about working for this band? How about you start with why you didn't mention it when we walked in."

"Are you going to grill me now?" I say, eyeing him with suspicion.

He stiffens, then takes a swig of his beer. "No, but it would be nice if you volunteered once in a while instead of me having to drag things out of you."

There are so many things—Corvus related stuff—that I haven't been able to share with him for so long, it just became second nature not to say much. I open my mouth to make up something random when an attractive redhead walks in through the main door and starts scanning the room.

Instead, I smile and dig into my pocket. Pulling out a piece of paper, I slide it across the table.

Samson follows my line of sight and squints at the girl. "She looks familiar," he mumbles, then glances down at the paper, confusion in his light blue eyes. "What is this?"

"*That* is her number," I say, waving to catch the redhead's attention. She smiles and as she makes her way toward us, I continue. "Her name's Emily Donovan. She's the nurse who took care of me at the hospital. Don't know what she sees in your sorry mug, but she asked me to give you her number."

When my brother starts to frown, I shake my head. "How long are you going to pretend not to care about dating? I don't want you to put your life on hold for me, Samson." Shrugging, I continue, "She's new here and doesn't know anyone, so since it's Christmas and all...I invited her to listen to the band with us."

"Hi, Ethan," she says once she reaches our table. "You look great. No lingering effects from your car accident?"

My brother's up and sliding a chair back before I get a chance to pull out one for her. I hold back a grin. His gaze hasn't left her face while she waits for my response. "I'm all good."

"I'm so glad to hear it." She glances Samson's way as she sits down. "Thank you, Samson. I'm Emily in case you forgot my name. It's good to see you again. I hope you don't mind me crashing your guy time, but Ethan texted and said to come and listen to this Weylaid band with you two. I'm a big music junkie."

Samson gives a half-laugh, then takes his seat. "My brother knows more about the band than I do. Apparently he's been working for them, doing equipment and such, for a while."

I ignore the dig in his tone and lean back in my chair, ready to listen to the band do their thing.

A half hour later, the bar's starting to fill up with people here to see Weylaid play. I'm enjoying the deep, rich sounds of the Southern rock music. Plus, it keeps me from having to watch my brother and Emily dance around their obvious mutual attraction. It occurs to me that with my brother completely distracted by Emily, now's a good time to talk to Matt, and since he likes Weylaid's sound, I send him a text inviting him to join us if he can.

A few minutes later, I get a text back from Matt saying he'll come in an hour. The latest song ends while I'm tucking my phone in my pocket. "We'll be back in five." The lead singer, Dom, lets the crowd know, but before he walks away from the mic, he points in my direction. "Hey Adder." He then curls his finger, calling me over.

I can't jump up fast enough. "I'll be back," I say to my brother. "Looks like they need me."

Samson waves me on without looking away from Emily.

I shake my head and move toward the side door. Bet he'll look up later and wonder where I went.

As soon as the door closes behind me, the whole band crowds into the hallway while Dom approaches, a wide grin on his face. "Tonight is really looking up. Ready to rock with us?"

"I can't play tonight, Dom. I'm here with my brother."

Dom smirks, raising a dark eyebrow. "Seems to me he's here with Red and you're a third wheel."

Even though I can't deny that very true statement, I open my mouth to make up some other excuse when Duke clasps me on the shoulder. "They need you to play lead guitar, Adder. I have to duck out early for a family event. Christmas Eve is the one time a year I can't bail. Chance here—" he tilts his head toward the blond musician leaning his head back against the wall with his eyes closed— "*really* appreciates your timely presence."

Chance doesn't even bother to open his eyes. "I'll personally consider it an early Christmas present."

"You really don't want to play?" I ask.

Chance shakes his head, his gaze finally meeting mine. "Not really. I can't improvise like you and Duke do. Been dreading this night all week until you showed up."

"We only have an hour left in the set," Dom says. "You don't have to play the after songs if you'd rather get back to your brother. What do you say?"

My brother is so completely into Emily, I doubt he'll even notice. I don't think he's looked at the stage once since she walked in. I slowly nod. "Just do me a favor and don't mention the switch up or announce me once we're on stage. Let's just play."

Dom shrugs. "Fine by me."

Duke shakes his shaggy red hair from his eyes and hands me his guitar. "Take care of her, dude."

Nodding, I take the instrument. When my hand folds around the neck and the strings push against the pads of my fingers, a sense of euphoria washes over me. It can't hurt to get lost in the music for a little while.

For the next hour, I bend over the guitar under the hot stage lights and revel in Adder's talent, enjoying the escape it brings. Even though I understand where my dreams come from now, I still wake up with my fists clenched and tension vibrating through me, so this release feels good.

While we move through rock songs, Southern rock and even a couple slower ballads, I let the pleasing sounds flow from my fingers up my arms, then down my body all the way to my tapping foot. All the while, I'm wishing I had the ability to take control of my dreams as easily as my fingers slide across these strings. I'm a bit jealous that Nara was somehow able to manipulate my own dream world while she was in it. Apparently, my brain is only wired to fight against the monsters, evil, and horrific scenarios that fill my sleep time, not eliminate them with a mere thought.

Should I blame the Corvus for my dreams? Up until now I believed the dark imagery was a manifestation of my mind working through the negative stuff I absorb from people I come in contact with, but maybe they're a result of both our strong minds and wills sharing the same space.

I just wish I could figure out how to stop the nightmares all together. Maybe if I work harder on mentally blocking the Corvus—there has to be a way, no matter what he says—I might be able to transfer that ability once I fall asleep.

The crowd's applause yanks me back to the here and now. I grip the guitar's neck and quickly lift my head to acknowledge all the whistles and calls for more.

Now that my senses are back, an awful stench hits me, making the burger in my stomach feel like a pound of wet cement.

Demons.

CHAPTER 12

ETHAN

ingers tightening on the guitar, my gaze narrows and I quickly scan the room for the source.

My line of sight stutters for a second when my eyes lock with my brother's. He's clapping along with the crowd, but the look on his face reflects more than surprise. His mouth is tense. He's hurt. Damn. I'd hoped to avoid—

An extra loud group of guys in the middle of the room pulls my attention away. All five are whooping and clapping and they're looking right at me. Every single one is a demon. While I see their demonic faces hiding behind the human bodies they're in, my mind races. *How do they know I'm Corvus?* Then I remember Nara telling me that Drake's Furia, the one who'd taken over David, told some Inferni about me. Of course they'd pick a public place to openly goad me.

I lock my jaw at the same time the Corvus inside me yanks my chin down, then jerks my head toward the main door, letting the bastards know he's ready when they are.

I don't disagree with the Corvus. I want the demons out of the bar and far away from everyone, especially my brother. I exhale a steadying breath, glad I took the stage when I did. It's better if the demons think I'm here alone.

I follow the band off the stage, but instead of hanging out in the back room with them afterward for some downtime, I tell them I need to get back out to my brother. Shutting the door behind me, I don't go to the bar. Instead, I clench my fists and turn down the hall, then take the door that leads into the alley.

The second I open the door, someone grabs my arm and yanks me outside into the dimly lit space between the buildings.

Stirred snow cakes the tops of my boots while all five demons quickly circle around me. I mentally call my sword, but my Corvus has other ideas. He casually kicks the snow off, then slowly pivots all the way around, tallying his adversaries; two Inferni have taken up residence inside older men, one is bald and the other has salt and pepper hair. The other three Inferni have taken over college-aged guys: a short one, a tall one, both with brown hair, and a skinny one with red hair. Once the Corvus has taken inventory, he smiles. My breath comes out in foggy gusts and my gut tightens; he's freaking smiling at them.

The arrogant bastard's enjoying the testosterone levels rising inside the demons, and while any other day I wouldn't mind a good fight, I don't have time for this shit. My brother could come looking for me any second.

Let me call my sword, damn you!

The Corvus makes a dismissive sound in my head. *Need I remind you of the deal we made about you letting me handle things? No one's around. These demon spawns are mine.*

Not this time. I have to get back to my brother—

Shut up and pay attention. You're about to get hit in the—

Pain splinters down my spine. One of the bastards—the skinny guy with red hair—hit the top of my shoulder with his fist, sneering in my ear, "Where's your sword, Corvus?"

Pressure wells inside me so fast I barely have time to think. My elbow slams my attacker in the throat, then I pivot and my fist hammers the bald guy's face. There's a fine line between my instinctual moves and the Corvus', but I can tell this is all him. The Corvus doesn't mess around.

My lip curls in satisfaction to see them both go down quickly. I know they won't be groggy for long, but it doesn't keep me from turning my back on them. I face the other three, fists raised. "Come on, Shitfernis. Give me your best sho—*oomph*"

The younger two rush me at the same time, jamming their shoulders into my chest.

I hit the Dumpster behind me hard, but when I remain on my feet and let out a low laugh, they jump back and cast each other a surprised look.

Even though my vision is slightly blurred, I vault across the alley, arms outstretched, clotheslining the bastards.

The instant both demons slam to the ground, I take advantage of the leverage their bodies give me and pull my feet forward, spring-boarding my boots off the on-coming demon's barrel chest. Curling into a backward flip, I land on the balls of my feet in the slick snow in time to see Mr. Salt and Pepper careen across the alley, his growls of fury cut off when he crashes into the opposite wall, sending brick pieces flying.

The Corvus chuckles. He's enjoying the violence. I can't help but laugh along with him. *Amateurs*, he mumbles in my head. The moment the thought enters my mind, I stumble forward in excruciating pain. The redhead has jumped on me, jamming his knees straight into my back. At the same time that he hooks an arm around my neck, he slams his fist into my jaw.

My head snaps sideways with the force, just as another demon roundhouse kicks me in the stomach. Air whooshes from my lungs and the sudden inability to breathe makes it hard to see, let alone focus on the knife's blade suddenly in my periphery.

A slicing sensation burns my arm and back, right before another demon joins in, landing a powerful kick into my side. *Pull your damn sword, Corvus!* I yell at the arrogant spirit inside me.

The Corvus jerks my hands up and grabs another foot swinging toward my jaw. With lightning speed, he twists the guy's leg so hard it snaps. While the older man crumples to the ground, groaning, the Corvus jerks my hand back and grabs the skinny guy's jacket collar, then tosses the guy off me with a flick of my wrist.

Happy? he snarls in my head.

I displace my anger at his blasé tone with a fist to the crotch of the guy closest to me. When he bends over to grab his injured junk, I knock away the long knife he used to slice my upper arm. Gritting my teeth through the biting pain in my bicep, I try to stand, but can't dodge in time to avoid the redhead's kick to my thigh. His steel-toed boot sends my knees back to the ground.

While the cold snow seeps into my jeans, the bald guy grabs my neck in another chokehold.

I growl and grab his arm, sheer fury ripping through me. I want to kill the Corvus right along with these guys. This might be his idea of fun, but the stupid spirit isn't the one getting treated like a punching bag.

And then everything goes black and all sounds cease. I stare and blink, but I can't see, hear or feel a thing.

"Ethan?"

The moment someone calls my name, my vision suddenly comes into focus. Along with my sight, the smell of blood and sweat invades my senses. Adrenaline still pumping through me, my breathing is labored and my body aches like hell, but every single demon around me is nursing at least one limb while trying to recover from my apparent ape-shit mode.

With black eyes, bloodied lips and swollen jaws, they drag themselves back up from the ground. Vengeance fills their battered faces, and they all lunge for me at once, fists flying.

"Hey, get off him!"

Everyone freezes for split second, then we all glance toward the top of the alley.

Matt's blond hair stands out in the dim light, worry flashing across his face. "Get off him, you bastards!"

A new level of tension builds inside me. *Shit. I forgot about Matt.*

"You know that guy?" The red-haired demon laughs, his gaze shifting to Matt, full of evil intent.

"Run, Matt," I yell, but of course he doesn't listen. The second Matt turns into the alley, I grab the guy's arm that's around my neck and shove his two-hundred-pound bulk back as if he weighs nothing. *The deal's off, Corvus. Now give me my—* My sword's in my hand before I finish the sentence. Straightening to my full height, I flip the sword backward and skewer the bald demon rushing me from behind.

When I look up, the redheaded demon has already knocked Matt to the ground, tossing him down like a piece of used tissue.

I let out a feral growl and yank the sword from the bald man, then spin and stab the tall dark-haired demon. Before the hobbling salt-and-pepper guy can react, I stab him too. While Matt groans and holds his hand to his head, the short dark-haired guy bolts to the redheaded demon's side.

As I approach in determined steps, my sword gripped in

my hand, they both step in front of Matt's crumpled body. They know he's their only leverage.

"You're welcome to try," I say in a cold tone, stopping a few feet away.

"You can't kill both of us before one of us snaps his puny body in half," the redhead leers, confident in his speed despite the fact his right arm hangs uselessly by his side.

I hold his gaze for a second, then give him a ruthless smile. "Which one of you wants to go back to Under first?"

The redhead flicks his eyes to the dark-haired demon. Before he can utter a word, I'm in his face, gripping his neck, my blade already plunged deep into the belly of the shorter one.

The gutted demon gasps in pain, his face reflecting shock. "Didn't even see me move, did you?" I say, satisfaction spiraling through me. Sensing just how nasty this one is through my sword's blade, I twist my blade and turn him into nothing but an explosion of moist particles. I'm happy to send him to Under for an extended stay.

The second his buddy is obliterated, the redhead uses his only good arm to pound against my arm, but his fist feels like cloth fluttering against me. My smile turns cold. "You messed with the wrong Corvus, demon."

He starts to tremble in my grip. "Don't send me back. He'll punish me."

I tilt my head, curious. I know when my sword sends them to Under, the veil wipes their memories of their time in the Mortal plane, but I didn't realize they retain their memories from Under when they make their way back. "You remember what happens to you while you're in Under?"

He nods. "He tortures those who get sent to Under now. Why do you think so many are fighting so hard to break through the veil? Here, we're gods. There we're given *incentive* to do whatever it takes to stay in the Mortal plane."

Sincerity reflects in his words, but viciousness and depravity oozes from every pore. It takes everything inside me not to snap his head clean off his body. "You should've thought about that before you jumped me." I jam my blade into his spineless body, a sense of justice rippling through me, but then I grumble my frustration. "You've got to be 'effing kidding me."

Unfortunately, my sword reveals the demon inside him has been hanging out in his body too long. This human's soul has been fully corrupted. Much as I'd like to send the Inferi to Under for a long ass stay, I can't obliterate the body too. Not without creating a Furia. Sliding my blade free, I grunt my disgust and release my hold, letting his unconscious body crumple to the ground.

Matt's groan draws me to his side. Setting my sword down, I help him sit up, then lean him against the brick wall. "Are you okay?"

He shakes his head for a second, his wide eyes jerking toward the alley. "What happened?"

I exhale slowly, relieved he apparently didn't see everything. "I guess my adrenaline kicked in once that guy knocked you down."

Matt rubs his temples, his gaze dropping to my sword. "That raven symbol. I've seen it before." Closing his eyes, he shakes his head, then opens them to stare at the blade once more.

"Where'd it go?" he asks, his disbelieving eyes returning to mine.

I feign ignorance. "Where'd what go?"

He gestures to my side. "There was a sword right beside you."

"That guy hit your head hard enough to knock you out for a minute. You're groggy, Matt."

"I saw it!" he insists, quickly scrambling to his feet. The

second he stands, he sees the unconscious redhead lying on the ground behind me. "That's him. That's the guy who came after me."

I grip Matt's arm, intending to lead him out of the alley. "I know. It's probably best we're not around when these guys come to."

Matt pulls free of my hold. "We should call the police. They attacked both of us." I turn to face him and Matt's eyes widen as I step into a sliver of light coming from a building across the mall. "You've been stabbed. Jesus, Ethan!"

I move the torn material back and glance at the cut on my arm. It'll be healed by tomorrow. "It's just a surface wound. Listen, Matt, I hit these guys hard enough to knock them out. I'd rather them not see us when they wake up. They could press charges."

"*We* should be pressing charges."

I shake my head. "It'll be their word against mine, and since they're all knocked out, it might not look so good for me."

He stares at the fallen guys and mumbles, "Wasn't there five of them?"

"No. Just four," I say, leading him away from the alley.

Matt looks like he wants to argue, but he lets me direct him back around to the front of McCormicks. Once we reach a pool of light near the main door, I say, "I think we should chalk this up to a life lesson about staying away from alleys."

"I saw a sword sitting in the snow beside you, Ethan." Matt spreads his hands wide in front of him. "It was about this long and it had a symbol on the blade near the hilt, the same one I've been seeing for a while. It's a raven yin-yang design."

I rub my jaw. "I'm familiar with that symbol and a

sword, but not a real one. What do you mean you've been seeing it for a while?"

His gaze narrows. "Tell me where the sword went first. Before I blacked out, I saw you use it on at least three—well, maybe it was two—of those guys. If you gutted them, how is it possible that they're still alive?"

I raise an eyebrow. "It was dark in the alley, and I had several guys jump me at once. One of them pulled a long knife. What you probably saw was *me* getting cut, not them."

A determined look crosses Matt's face. "I saw what I saw, Ethan. I might've blacked out for a minute, but when I opened my eyes again, you were squatting next to me, and that sword was on the ground beside you."

I wrack my brain and decide appealing to his logical side is the best course. "If the sword was on the ground, where did it go? You would've seen me pick it up. Did you?"

My question draws a frown from Matt, doubt creeping into his eyes for the first time. "I—didn't see you pick it up." Sighing, he pushes a shaky hand through his short hair. "I've seen that symbol before."

I quickly turn and pull my shirt up so he can see the sword tattoo on my back. "This is probably where you've seen it, and maybe even where you got a sword idea in your head. You must've seen me changing in gym."

"I guess it's possible I saw it while passing you in the locker room during class change over. Though I think I would've stopped and stared. That's a lot of ink. An impressive tattoo for sure." When I lower my shirt and turn back around, he asks, "What does that symbol mean?"

"It represents balance and protection."

His blond eyebrows pull together. "That's good, right? So why have I been seeing it flash through my head? Well, what I see is similar, but not exactly the same. In my mind, the symbol used to look like the one on your tattoo. Then later, I saw the black bird breaking into hundreds of smaller birds. For a while I saw both images, but lately it's just the second one."

"You said the image flashed through your head. How long have you been seeing it?"

He exhales, his breath stuttering out. "The past couple of months."

A couple months? A group of people walk up behind us, so I pull Matt off to the side and say in a low voice, "Do you remember when you started seeing the image?"

Matt squints, sifting through his memory. "It wasn't long after Drystan came to live with us. I remember because I wanted to tell him but was too freaked out about it." His expression tenses once more. "I've tried to research the symbol, but nothing pops up on the web. All I know is... each time I saw it in my mind, I felt compelled to draw it. The whole experience was so out there, I didn't tell anyone about my drawings, but Lainey happened to see one and asked me about it. She's the only person I've shared this obsession with until you." His face tenses. "It's driving me crazy that I keep seeing it."

I put my hand on his shoulder to calm him down. "Lainey said you planned to get a tattoo."

"Yeah. I asked an artist buddy of mine if he'd do it for me. He's doing tattoos on the side. The guy's talent is through the roof. I didn't tell him about the imagery, visions...whatever it is. Do you think if I got it inked..." He pauses and swallows. "That maybe the image I keep seeing will go away?"

I shake my head. "I don't know what the symbol you've been seeing means. Regardless if it makes the vision stop, I do know that the one on my back gives a level of protection. If you're going to get a tattoo, get that one."

Matt nods, his expression resigned. "Lainey told me that

I should consider where I get it done so I don't lock myself out of certain jobs later."

I release him and offer a half smile. "Yeah. Good point."

A group of people walk out of McCormicks, cutting off our conversation. I nod toward the door. "You want to come inside and listen to the band? They'll be playing a few more songs soon before packing up for the night. I'll be here for another half hour, then I have to be at Nara's by seven-thirty."

Matt grins. "That's why I'm here."

I turn and open the door. "Good. I'll have someone to talk to while my brother completely ignores me for the new girl in his life."

"You came here on a date with your brother?" Matt follows me inside, laughing.

I shake my head. "No. I invited Emily tonight because she's new in town and she'd asked for my brother's number before. She was the nurse who took care of me at the hospital."

As we wind our way to the table and Matt sees where we're headed, he nods toward Samson and Emily and mutters under his breath, "Their chairs are pretty close together. I'd say they're getting to know each other *real* well."

I snort, then step up to the table, grabbing my jacket off the back of my chair. "Hey, Samson and Emily." I try not to wince as I quickly shrug into my coat to cover the wound on my arm. My ribs definitely took a beating tonight. What the hell happened while I blacked out? I don't like the fact that I lost a chunk of time. Just when I say, "This is my friend, Matt," the lights go down and Weylaid starts playing. I have to raise my voice to be heard over the music. "He's going to hang with us for a bit."

Once Emily shakes Matt's hand, her attention quickly

shifts to me. "That was some amazing guitar playing, Ethan. Thanks for inviting me."

I nod and mumble my thanks. I feel my brother's heavy gaze on me, but I refuse to look at him. He's going to rip into me when we're alone. Even though I don't drink, a beer sounds really good right now. Unfortunately, ordering one would probably send Samson off the deep end, so I turn my chair toward the stage and settle in for more music.

A half hour later, snow coats our hair as my brother and I head toward the deck after he walked Emily to her car parked on a side street. I'm surprised he hasn't said anything to me yet, but I'm not saying anything to disturb the peaceful silence between us.

We're almost to parking deck before Samson finally speaks. "Were you ever planning on telling me?"

I dig my hands a bit deeper into my jean pockets. "It's no big deal."

"No big— you mean like the cut on your brow?"

I tense, feeling defensive. "Some guys were trying to mess with Matt when I went outside to meet him. I jumped in to—"

"How is it that I had no idea you played?" my brother cuts in, saying what's really on his mind.

I shrug, but refuse to look at him when we enter the parking deck stairwell. "I just picked it up recently."

"Recently? Ethan, you played like someone who's been playing all his *life*."

"Yeah, it just came to me." I skip up the stairs ahead of him. Opening the door to the floor we're parked on, I hold it until he follows me out. "I can't really explain it any better than that."

Samson shakes his head. "You still should've shared."

I lift my eyebrows. "Does this mean you're going to share why you got so mad at Mom and Dad earlier?"

He frowns, then turns to walk toward his car.

That's what I thought. I quickly fall into step beside him, a half smile on my lips. "So, you going to ask Emily out?"

We've almost reached his car, when my brother clamps his hand on the back of my neck. Yanking me toward him, he curls his muscular arm around my neck, then knuckle-noogies the top of my head, driving the snow into my scalp. "You're going to tell me next time, right?"

"Yes," I snort out, trying not to laugh. He hasn't done this since I was a kid.

Without a word, he releases me and moves to his side of the car.

Shaking my head, I grab my door handle and stare at him over the roof. "Well?"

He laughs. "Yeah, we're going to dinner next week. Now get in the car and quit grilling me."

CHAPTER 13

NARA

"I don't understand why you're coming to get me so early," Gran says while I help her into my car. A quarter inch of snow has already coated my windshield in the time it took for me to sign in at the front desk at Westminster's retirement community and knock on Gran's door. "This steady snow is supposed to turn into a blizzard later," I say before I shut her door. I'm glad I left early and reburied Freddie's book by his graveside for safekeeping before coming to get Gran. With this bad weather, it might be a few days before I could get back out to the cemetery.

Gran's riffling through the recyclable grocery bag she's set on the floor by her feet as I slide into my side of the car. "It's a good thing I brought this," she says, holding something up with a wide grin.

I snicker at the thin tool and start my car. "A screwdriver?"

"What?" Confusion deepens the wrinkles on her face. "Oh, not that." She quickly drops the tool back into her bag and rummages through it once more before pulling out a toothbrush. "If the weather's as bad as they say it's going to be, I'm prepared. The last time I stayed over, you had to open a new brush for me."

"Ah..." I nod my understanding, and she tucks her toothbrush back into her bag. I'm almost afraid to ask, but I do anyway. "Why do you carry a screwdriver in your purse?"

"Who doesn't?" Gran says, looking at me like I should know better. "It's like duct tape. Comes in handy for so many things."

I chuckle and shake my head. "I'll um, take your word for it, Gran."

Patting her curled hair, she sighs. "I don't know why I bothered to go to the beauty salon. The snow is going to ruin my fancy hairdo." Setting her hands in her lap, she narrows her gaze on me. "Okay, now tell me the real reason you're picking me up early."

The real reason is...it's all my fault Mom's running around in super angst mode. I shrug. "Mom wants your help preparing dinner."

Gran makes a harrumph sound. "She wants my help or she needs my help?"

"Same thing."

"No, it's not, dear." My great aunt chuckles. "Your mom might *need* my help with the meal, but I guarantee you she's not going to ask for it. She's definitely her mother's daughter in this case; my sister could be very stubborn. So why is Elizabeth suddenly a titter over a meal? For someone who balances numbers all day, she sure can't follow a recipe to save her life. It's like she sees the measurements as suggestions. If she wants to impress her new man, she should save the improvisation for other activities—like trapeze pole dancing."

Shaking my head to get rid of the sudden disturbing image of my mom twirling half-naked around a slowly swinging pole, I can't help but snicker as I turn onto the highway. "It's not about the food, Gran." I casually glance her way. "Dad's coming to dinner with Aunt Sage."

Gran's gray eyebrows shoot high. "Really? And the plot thickens. How did that happen?"

I wait for traffic to clear out of the way before merging into another lane. "I recently reconnected with Dad, and as a favor to me, I asked Mom to invite him since she'd already invited Aunt Sage."

Gran pins me with a surprised look. "That was awfully brave of you, Inara."

Grimacing, I fold my fingers like a vise around the steering wheel. "Yeah well, the only reason Mom agreed is because David was also coming."

"That makes a bit more sense, I suppose," Gran says, bobbing her gray head.

"There's just one slight problem." I cast a furtive look her way. "David called to cancel an hour ago. He doesn't feel well." I had been the one to answer the phone when he called. Instead of asking to speak to Mom, he told me that he's still not feeling himself after what happened yesterday and asked me to tell my mom that he's just not feeling well. Guilt knotted my stomach once I hung up the phone. I'm still not sure if Mr. Dixon cancelling was a temporary thing, or if he just couldn't handle yesterday's craziness and was distancing himself.

"So, it's just going to be you, your mom, Sage, Jonathan, and me?"

Gran's question snaps my attention back to her. "My boyfriend, Ethan, is coming too, so you'll finally get to meet him."

Flashing me a quick smile, she tilts her head and asks, "Does Jonathan still love your mom?"

"Yes," I say, then bite my lip and wait for the judgment of

my dad's choices and utter lack of respect for my mom to fly from her lips.

Gran cackles and slaps her thigh. "This is going to be better than any of those soap operas on TV."

I'm so shocked, all I can do is wait until she gets control of her laughter. "You're not mad at him?"

Gran shrugs. "You saw past whatever reason he had for leaving. That's good enough for me."

If only Mom could trust my instincts like Gran does. While some of the tightness eases from my shoulders, Gran says, "I'm too old to carry grudges, sweetie. That's way too much baggage to haul around in my advanced years. I leave all that heavy stuff to the youngins. I know your mom is going to give that man holy hell. I almost feel sorry for him."

With her last sentence, I sigh.

Fifteen minutes later, when we start to walk through the front door, Gran grabs my arm and points to the mistletoe in the top of the doorway. "Can't mess with tradition."

Tugging her bag up on my shoulder, I grin and bend down for her to kiss my cheek. "I had no idea you were so superstitious, Gran."

She pecks my cheek, then pats it with her gnarled hand. "Your grandmother had her obsession with ravens, I have mine, dear."

"Which is?" I ask, raising an eyebrow.

"Never you mind," she says, winking.

"Corda, I'm so glad you could come," Mom calls from the top of the stairway, her voice a bit higher than usual. She has also changed clothes from the ones she had on before I left to get Gran.

Oh, yeah...she's stressed.

As my mom descends the stairs, Houdini thumps down the steps at rapid speed beside her, Gran follows me inside and snickers in my ear as I shut the door, "Yep, it's going to be an entertaining evening for sure."

"Shhhh, Gran," I say in a low voice, then immediately tell my mom as she approaches, "The snow is coming down harder now. The roads are getting messy."

Slight relief filters across her face. "Oh, well, it might just be the three of us then."

When Gran bursts out laughing—if she were Lainey, Drystan or Ethan, she'd be getting an elbow in the ribs, but Gran's pushing eighty—I shake my head and tell Mom, "Gran's in rare form tonight."

Nodding her acknowledgment that Gran is having one of her loopy moments, Mom's gaze drops to the bag on my shoulder. "Why don't you put Corda's stuff in her room and then you can help me set the table."

"Take the gifts from my bag and put them under the tree first," Gran says.

I follow Gran's instructions, then head upstairs. Just when I start down the stairs, the doorbell rings. Of course Houdini rushes forward barking, but Mom is quick to pull him back and open the door.

Holding a handled shopping bag, Ethan is standing there in jeans, a black sweater and a leather bomber jacket. "Merry Christmas, Mrs. Collins."

"Mer—Merry Christmas, Ethan." Mom pulls the door wide and stands back for him to come in.

Mom has paused for a reason, and when I greet him, I see why. He has a deep cut along the edge of his eyebrow. "Are you okay?" I step forward, searching his face.

He shrugs and stomps the snow off his boots. "I'm good. Caught the corner of the cabinet when I bent over to toast some bread earlier."

Before he can take a step inside, Gran tuts, "Uh, ah."

Wagging her finger, she points to the mistletoe. "Follow tradition, young man."

Ethan flashes Gran a wide smile before he turns to me and drops a chaste, but sweet kiss on my lips, saying in that sexy, low voice of his, "I like your Gran already."

I rub my arms and mumble about his mouth being cold to cover the fact I just shuddered in response to his kiss. Even though I'm worried about the real reason he got that cut, my body still reacts to his incredibly warm mouth pressing against mine for the briefest of seconds.

Once Mom shuts the door behind Ethan and I officially introduce him to Gran, I turn to him. "Can you come upstairs and help me bring down my gifts? We usually open them right after dinner."

After Ethan shrugs out of his jacket and then follows me into my room, I turn and start to say, "What happe—"

But he steps close and clasps my jaw, pressing his mouth against mine. I curl my fingers into the hem of his sweater and melt against him, kissing him back.

A few seconds later, he lifts his head and wraps his arms around my waist, pressing a soft kiss to my forehead. *"That's the kind of kiss I wanted to give you under that mistletoe."*

I giggle that he sounds so disgruntled and start to peck a kiss on his jawline when I pause at the sight of slight bruising under his skin there. I gingerly touch his jaw. "What happened?"

Ethan cups his warm hand over mine. "It's no biggie. The demons Drake's Furia sent my way finally found me."

"Demons?" My eyes widen. "How many?"

He shrugs. "Just five."

"Five." My voice hikes and I quickly lower it. "Five? Oh God, Ethan."

Clasping my shoulders, he shakes his head. "I'm fine, Nara. They're all taken care of. I'm just glad they didn't jump me while I was with my brother. Matt almost got caught in the crossfire, but thankfully he didn't see much. He just got banged up a little bit."

I gape. "Matt saw you fighting? How did he get hurt?"

"It was dark in the alley beside McCormicks—Samson and I went there after the disaster that was supposed to be our family dinner. Don't ask. Anyway, Matt stumbled across the demons attacking me and got knocked out. He did see my sword, but I convinced him that he was seeing things since he woke up groggy."

"So he's alright?" When he nods, I exhale my relief. "Did you get a chance to talk to him about the image he's been seeing?"

Ethan nods. "Yeah, him seeing my sword gave me an idea how he might've seen the raven yin-yang symbol before we officially met. Our gym classes are back to back, so it's entirely possible that he might've subconsciously seen it while I was getting dressed, then recalled it later. At least that's what I suggested to him."

"And he bought that?"

Shrugging, he chuckles. "It is possible, and it's a far easier pill to swallow than to believe he's losing his mind. I convinced him to get a tattoo like the one on Lainey's locket instead of the one in his head."

"Did you learn anything about why he's seeing the image in the first place?"

He sighs. "The only thing he told me that I found interesting was the timing of when he started seeing the image. He said it wasn't long after Drystan came to live with him."

I blink. "You don't think Drystan is the cause of what he's seeing, do you?"

"I don't know what to think, but you have to admit the timing is a little too coincidental."

I nod and bite my lip. "I agree it's odd timing, but I'm

pretty sure Drystan had never seen the symbol before he met me. Matt seeing it may have nothing to do with Drystan at all."

I can tell by his expression Ethan doesn't like the scenario I'm implying—that I might be the source of Matt's vision. Grunting his frustration, he pulls me close and folds his arms tightly around my waist. "At least I convinced Matt to get the right tattoo if he insists on getting one. Eventually we'll figure out what the image in his head means."

I rest my head on his shoulder for a few seconds and hug him back. Glancing at the bag he set by the doorway, I sigh and say, "Ready to help me bring down my gifts?"

Ethan gestures to the bag. "That is part of your gifts."

I tilt my head, eyeing him. "Huh? You brought those."

He looks serious as he retrieves the bag and opens it for me to see inside. "These are all gifts for your family, Nara."

My attention snaps from the small wrapped boxes in the bag to him. "Why did you get gifts for my family?"

He smiles. "That was a great gift you gave Lainey. Apparently you and I had the same goal in mind this Christmas—doing what we can to protect the people in our lives."

I gesture to the boxes. "But that's too much. The money you spent on these gifts could've gone toward the school trip to London."

He hands me the bag and shakes his head. "This is more important. I want you to give these gifts to your family as if they're from you."

"But...why?" I try to hand him the bag back, but he just shakes his head.

"If they come from you, your family will be more likely to wear them all the time."

I press my lips together, knowing he's right. Gratitude tightens my chest and my fingers curl around the bag's handles. "I struggled with what I should get my dad, but finally settled on a wallet with a metal money clip on it. The symbol is underneath the clip."

"Sneaky." Ethan looks proud. "You can give him that present tomorrow. Tonight you're giving him a watch. The symbol is on the back."

Smiling, I lean close and kiss his jaw. "Thank you."

"Nara." Mom steps into the doorway of my room, her hand on the top button of the tailored jacket she's wearing. "This jacket's bothering me, so I'm changing. Can you go down and entertain Corda? I might be a little bit."

"Okay, Mom. Did Aunt Sage say when they're coming?"

"She just said she'd be a little late. My guess is fifteen minutes."

After she walks away, I shake my head. "Did you notice she didn't say 'they'?"

He slowly nods his agreement. "Come on, let's put your presents in this bag and go hang with your Gran."

"That's a big present," Gran says from her seat on the couch while I slide David's gift beside the ones from Ethan and me that are under the tree.

"It's from David," I say and step back. "He dropped it off yesterday and asked me to hide it." I tilt my chin toward the stairwell, then continue, "I'm going to tell Mom he dropped it off just now while she was upstairs."

Gran folds her hand in her lap. "Why?"

I shrug. "Because it'll make her feel better."

"She's fine." Gran snorts and waves her hand.

"No, she's not. That's the third time she has changed clothes that I *know* of," I say, pursing my lips.

Gran starts to say something when the doorbell rings. Mom calls from upstairs, "I'll be right down, Inara."

Gran clasps her hands in front of her chest, her green eyes sparkling. "Let the entertainment begin."

Ethan lets out a surprised laugh, and I just shake my head and give him a small smile. "Welcome to my slightly off-kilter family."

Once I pull open the door and greet my aunt and father, Houdini instantly presses his big head to my dad's thigh.

"Hey boy!" he says, patting his head, then scratching his ear.

Gran nudges Houdini out of the way and steps into place by my side, her presence somehow balancing the chaotic emotions flowing through me.

"Hello again, Sage dear." Before my aunt can even respond, Gran looks at my dad and continues in the same light tone, "Well, that was a heck of a trip you took, Jonathan. I hope you brought exceptional presents to make up for your extended party-of-one vacation."

When Ethan coughs behind me, I know he's reacting to Gran's forthright dig, but I keep my focus on my dad, whose smile looks frozen on his face.

"It's good to see your sense of humor is still sharp and on-point as always, Corda," he says in an even tone.

"Everything else might be failing like an old clunker ready for the junkyard, but," Gran taps her temple. "This engine's still roaring, young man. Don't you forget it."

My father inclines his head in acknowledgement. "I wouldn't expect anything less."

"Come in," I say, taking the shopping bag from my aunt's hand. "You can put your boots on the rubber mat by the door."

Before they step inside, Gran points above their heads. "Pay attention to the mistletoe, you two."

Aunt Sage grins and kisses her brother on the cheek. "Merry Christmas, Jonathan."

My father laughs, then steps inside, unraveling the scarf from his neck. "What's that cooking? It smells good."

After Sage closes the door behind them, Mom says from her position halfway down the stairs, "Pot roast and vegetables. Merry Christmas and welcome. Inara, please take our guests' coats so they can be comfortable."

I don't miss the fact that Mom's treating my father like a guest in his own home. Technically he is, but it still feels weird. I ignore the tightening of my dad's jawline and paste on a smile as I wish my aunt a Merry Christmas.

Once Aunt Sage hands me her coat, then steps forward to thank my mom for inviting them, I wait for my dad to take his off. While he shrugs out of it, he glances Ethan's way and says in a brisk tone, "You must be Ethan."

I glance at my dad, confused for a second, then remember that my mom has no idea he's already met Ethan.

Ethan follows his cue and holds out his hand to shake my dad's. "Nice to meet you, Mr. Collins."

Dad's gaze locks on the cut on Ethan's brow for a couple beats before he releases his hand and smiles at me. "Merry Christmas, Nari." When he steps close like he's going to hug me, I catch my Mom pretending not to watch us from the kitchen and wave my hand for his coat. "Merry Christmas. I'll take that, then you can check out the kitchen. We have warm spicy tea or eggnog if you'd like some."

Dad nods, then bends close when he hands me his coat and scarf, whispering in my ear, "Sage told me Ethan has horrible dreams all the time. Why am I not surprised to find out he's estranged from his parents?"

Of course he focuses on the negative. My fingers folding tight around his coat and I whisper back in a sharp tone, "And, on the surface, you look like a deadbeat, deserter father."

Dad jerks upright, frowning. As he mumbles a tight-lipped, "Touché," Gran walks up behind me.

"Ooh, is there rum in the eggnog? Jonathan, come and

pour me a cup. These old hands aren't as steady as they used to be."

Nodding to Gran, my father pats Houdini's head once more, then follows her into the kitchen where Aunt Sage is already helping Mom set out the appetizers.

While I hang my dad and my aunt's coats, Ethan moves to my side and says in a low voice, "Your father doesn't like me much, does he?"

I'm so glad Ethan didn't hear what he said. I hadn't planned to say something so harsh to my dad, but hopefully he'll get that things aren't always as they seem, and he'll ease off on his blanket judgment. Unfortunately, as much as I'd like to tell my father the truth about Ethan, doing so wouldn't help my case at all. I'm pretty sure it would just make my dad even more protective. Draping my father's scarf along the collar of his coat, I glance at Ethan over my shoulder. "My dad just doesn't know you very well yet. Give him some time."

Ethan releases the bit of hair that had stuck to my lip gloss when I turned to look at him. Sliding his fingers slowly down the blonde strands, his deep blue gaze holds mine. "All I care about is what you think."

I look at his injured eyebrow and the barely noticeable bruising along his jaw. "I know you can't help what finds you, but all I ask is that you don't go looking for trouble."

His lips twitch. "I've got enough trouble on my hands without seeking it out."

My heart twinges slightly, but I nod and murmur, "Okay then, ready for an interesting dinner?"

Ethan rests his hand on the small of my back and answers in a low tone, "Here's hoping the mistletoe's power extends beyond doorways. Then again, your Gran's a force all on her own. I think we've got the bases covered."

His dry comment makes me smile. Though I'm never

exactly sure where Gran's going with half the things she says, she somehow manages to dispense her own brand of wisdom along the way. Having Ethan here, too, with his warm, solid presence by my side makes me believe in the possibility that everything will work itself out.

CHAPTER 14

NARA

*T*hen again, maybe things will never be right again, I think to myself after watching my father try several times during dinner to engage my mother. Honestly, he got more attention and admiration from Houdini, who did the rounds at the table but always ended up at my father's side, resting his chin on his thigh.

My mom spent the entire meal being the perfect hostess. She smiled when she should. Cracked a few jokes, and she even laughed at Aunt Sage's funny stories about she and my dad as children. In essence, Mom radiated utter calm and holiday happiness.

Gran was unusually quiet, watching their mannerly conversation like a ping-pong match. I missed her barbs and crazy sayings.

Neither of my parents talked about the past. At all. It's like they never had one and I was born out of thin air.

Ethan must've felt my pain, because he uncurled my vice hold on my thigh under the table and laced our hands together instead. I ate the entire meal with my left hand, but

I didn't care. I wasn't giving up the connection and support he offered for anything.

Now that dinner's over, I actually breathe a sigh of relief when Gran claps her hands and says, "Okay, dinner's done. Let's open presents." Looking pointedly at Mom, Gran continues, "Take Jonathan and Sage into the living room, while the youngest and oldest clear off the table."

"I can't let you do that," Mom starts to say, then clamps her lips shut when Gran shoots her a pointed look.

Chuckling softly, Mom gives the first genuine smile I've seen all night. "That's the same look my mom used to give me." She stands and gestures for my father and my aunt to do the same. "You heard Corda. Let's give them space to clean up."

Ethan and I do most of the heavy lifting while Gran sneaks another cup of eggnog and sips on it each time she returns to the kitchen with a plate to scrape off. I snicker at Gran and roll my tight shoulders as some of the tension eases.

We are just about to leave the kitchen and join the others in the living room, when I look up to see Houdini with an entire bunch of mistletoe in his mouth. "No, Houdini!" Ethan and I chase him around the island a couple of times before we trap him in the corner. He stares at us with big brown eyes full of mischief, like he's enjoying the chase. "Let it go, Houdini," I say as calmly as I can, even though I'm worried to death. Ugh, it must've fallen from the doorway to the garage. The leaves can be pretty toxic to animals too. Houdini twitches his ears, but doesn't release the greenery. I'm afraid to jerk it out of his mouth. A smaller piece might break off that he can swallow.

Ethan steps close and touches Houdini's head, commanding gently, "Release it, boy. That's not good for you." And just like that, Houdini drops the entire bunch on the floor at Ethan's feet.

Grabbing up the mistletoe, I set it on the counter and exhale a sigh of relief. "That was close."

Ethan smiles and pats Houdini's head. "Catastrophe avoided."

When we finally join the others in the living room, my aunt hands me a small box she pulls from the bag she brought with her. "Merry Christmas, Inara."

"Thank you, Aunt Sage." Holding the gift from my aunt, I gather the ones Ethan had brought for my family and pass them all out at once, saying, "Since this is kind of a themed gift, I want you all to open yours at the same time first."

As I settle on the arm of the wingback chair Ethan's sitting in, my family opens their gifts.

"Very pretty, Inara. The detail is so intricate," Mom says, holding up a nickel-sized silver locket necklace with the Corvus symbol engraved inside.

"Here, let me help you put it on," I say, stepping forward to clasp it around her neck. Once Mom's is done, I step away to help Aunt Sage put hers on.

Touching her charm, Aunt Sage stares at Mom's matching one. "Thank you. It's very unusual. I love the ravens. It's a shame they're hidden away in the locket."

I smile. "Ethan helped me pick the gifts out. Hiding them is what makes it a good luck charm. Wearing the locket will always keep you safe."

"Can you help me, dear?" Gran fumbles trying to put hers on. I catch the silver-dollar-sized Corvus broach before it reaches her lap. Gran's ravens are hidden behind an intricate branches and leaves design. Pinning it to her red cardigan, I step back and smile. "It looks perfect on you, Gran."

She grins. "It's lovely, Inara. Clara is going to be so jealous."

"Thank you, Nari," my father says, holding up his new watch to inspect the symbol on the back.

When my father's gaze zeros on Ethan's back while Ethan leans over to help stuff some wrapping paper in a trash bag, I tense. Ethan's sweater has ridden up and part of his sword tattoo is showing. It's bad enough my dad now knows Ethan has a sword tattoo, but does he remember seeing the raven symbol on Ethan's sword in that dream we all shared? My father would've had to really stare at the weapon to have seen it, and as far as I recall, Ethan was moving pretty quickly each time he had seen him holding it.

"It's just great to see you embracing Margaret's passion," Gran says, full of nostalgia. I glance her way to see her absently rubbing her fingers across the broach. "She really did love ravens."

"I remember Mom focusing on ravens in all those art classes you two took together," Mom says, smiling. "I just saw the statue she sculpted in Inara's room the other day. Thank you for saving it for her. It's like a piece of my mom is still here with us."

I flick a stop-being-so-judgy gaze to my father, who reluctantly slides his attention from Ethan to wrap the watch's leather band around his wrist.

"Open yours," Aunt Sage says, her hazel eyes brimming with excitement.

I quickly rip open the ribbon and wrapping and gasp at the half-carat diamond earrings. "Aunt Sage, this is too much."

She gestures to my dad. "It's from both of us. Put them on and let us see your shiny lobes."

As I quickly slip the earrings on, I notice my mom's pinched lips.

Standing, she bends down and retrieves a slim gift box

from under the tree, then hands it to me. "Might as well give you this now."

I furrow my brow. We usually exchange our gifts in the morning time. "Are you sure, Mom?"

Nodding, she offers a wry half-smile then sits back down beside Gran.

When I pull off the gift paper and open the jewelry box, Mom says, "Now you'll have a matching set."

I lift up the necklace with a solitaire diamond. "Wow, great minds. It's like you guys were in sync or something."

"I guess," Mom says, then motions me to her so she can put the necklace on. Once it's done, she touches the diamond around my neck. "Merry Christmas, Inara."

I can tell she's feeling a bit one-upped by my aunt and dad, so I hug her tight. "Thank you, Mom. I love it so much." When she hugs me back harder than she ever has, I whisper in her ear, "Nothing will ever change between us. I love you."

Mom's a little teary when I straighten, but her smile is back. She squeezes my hands and we exchange a look of understanding.

"It's lovely, Inara," Aunt Sage says, lightening the heavy mood that has descended around us.

When I turn to thank her, Gran points to the big box under the tree. "Open your gift from David, Elizabeth."

Mom's eyes widen. "That's from David?"

Gran nods. "Yup. He dropped it off while you were upstairs changing and insisted you open it tonight so he could be here in spirit."

"Maybe I should wait," Mom starts to say, but Gran shakes her head.

"No, he *insisted*, dear. Open it."

While I move to sit back with Ethan, I glance at Gran, my eyebrows raised. She just embellished the heck out of the story I'd planned to tell Mom about the gift under the tree. And why is she pushing Mom to open it now?

"That was sweet of him to bring it by considering he's sick." Mom's eyes light up and she moves to squat next to the gift.

My father straightens his spine a bit, his jaw hardening while Mom tears into the gift. When he smirks slightly and says, "He bought you a crockpot?" it's hard not to roll my eyes at him.

I quickly point to the crockpot box. "David said the real gift is inside, Mom."

"Oh, okay." Mom pulls an annoyed look from my father's direction and opens the box.

When she lifts out an envelope, I smile. "Open it."

Mom flips back the flap and lifts out the official looking card, then presses her lips together.

"Well, what is it?" Gran asks, eyes brimming with curiosity as she leans over to see. "Oh, it's a gift certificate for cooking lessons."

As Gran makes a *hmmm* sound, my dad mutters, "Winning lots of points there."

My aunt cuts a sharp look to her brother at the same time my mom narrows her gaze on him for a split second. Sliding the box and envelope back under the tree, Mom stands and spreads her hands. "Who would like some eggnog?"

While Mom makes a fast retreat to the kitchen, Gran grabs the envelope once more, her brow furrowed. Waving it in the air, she said, "Did you read David's note, Elizabeth?"

Mom pauses in pouring some rum into her cup of eggnog, her expression a bit anxious. "There was a note?"

Gran holds the card up, glances at my dad for a brief second, then reads out loud, "My dearest Elizabeth, I'm looking forward to taking these classes with you. To me, the best part will be a chance to spend some quality time together. Merry Christmas. David." Lowering the card, Gran grins. "Aw, now that's sweet."

Mom beams, her entire face transforming.

Dad scowls and my aunt covers her mouth, trying not to laugh at him. Gran turns toward my father. "What'd you get her, Jonathan?"

He starts to reach into the bag Aunt Sage brought in with them, but Houdini makes a horrific retching sound, grabbing all our attention. I jump up and herd my dog to the kitchen's tile floor, worry sliding through me.

Houdini manages to stop retching, but then he looks at the door and starts whining pitifully.

My father approaches with the leash in his hand. "I'll take him out." He has already put on his coat, so I hook the leash on Houdini's collar and hand him the looped end. "Thanks, Dad."

A few minutes later, Dad comes back in with Houdini. Both are covered in snow and Houdini is quivering all over. "Where's the nearest vet clinic?" Dad asks, his expression tense.

"What happened?"

"He threw up several times."

I tense with worry. "Oh God, what if the mistletoe poisoned him?"

Ethan squats and rubs Houdini's snout, then stands and clasps my hand. "He's not a happy camper right now, that's for sure."

I move to get my coat off the rack, but my dad shakes his head. "The storm has gotten worse, Nari. I could barely see three feet in front of me out there. I'll drive him. Just tell me where an emergency clinic is that'll be open on Christmas Eve."

"It's that bad out there?" Aunt Sage asks.

"I know where a clinic is," Mom says, grabbing her coat.

"I pass it every day on the way to work. I'll take you or you'll never find it."

My attention darts between my parents, thoughts of them fighting while they try to deal with Houdini pinging through my head. "I can take him, Mom."

"You're not driving in this, Inara." She quickly wraps her scarf around her neck, then waves dismissively. "Houdini will be fine."

My dad looks at his sister. "You might want to leave now too before the roads become impassable. You can't get stuck here with three dogs waiting for you at home. I'll catch a cab once we get back."

Nodding her agreement, Aunt Sage hugs me goodbye, then puts on her boots and coat.

My father gives Ethan a pointed look. "You should leave now too."

Gran puckers her lips as if she's eaten something sour. "The boy hasn't had a chance to exchange presents with Nara yet, Jonathan."

My dad frowns. "He might get stuck here if he doesn't leave now—"

"I can walk home if I need to," Ethan says, squeezing my hand.

"What am I? Chopped suey?" Gran says, pointing to herself. "I'm a better watch dog than Houdini. He does whatever Ethan tells him."

When my dad's face hardens even more at Gran's last comment, Mom cuts in, her tone final. "You can stay and exchange gifts with Nara, Ethan. No one's rushing you out."

"Go take care of the pooch." Gran waves my parents on. "I'm sure he'll be fine. That plant was in his mouth less than a minute. It's probably all the pot roast I fed him under the table. It was a bit tough on my dentures."

"But you asked for seconds," Mom says, looking incredulous.

Gran shrugs. "Houdini seemed to enjoy it."

When Mom sighs and shakes her head, Gran pats her arm. "The cooking lessons aren't a bad idea, dear. If I tried to teach you, everything would have rum in it."

Once my parents leave with Houdini, Aunt Sage wishes Gran a Merry Christmas and hugs her goodnight. Turning to me, my aunt pulls me into a tight hug, then glances at Ethan. "Thank you for the gift."

He shakes his head, nodding toward me. "It was from Nara."

She just smiles and says, "Mmmm, hmmm."

The second the door shuts behind my aunt, Gran does a little hop, then makes a bee-line straight for the bag Aunt Sage left by the couch.

When she withdraws an envelope and starts to pull open the tucked in flap, I say, "You can't open that, Gran. And what's with torturing Mom and Dad over the presents?"

"I got tired of watching them be polite to each other all through dinner. It was like watching two eggs roll into each other over and over. When neither cracked, I decided to crank up the heat and poach their brains."

She shrugs, unrepentant, then looks down at the envelope, folding the flap all the way back. "Don't you want to know what your father brought for your mother? I'm not getting any younger. Gotta get my kicks while I still can." She reads the contents, then looks up, her green eyes glittering with emotional mist.

"What does it say?" I ask, my stomach tensing in anticipation.

She lifts the paperwork and reads the card on the front. "For all the anniversaries I missed. I hope this trip gives us plenty of time to catch up. I love you, Elizabeth. I never

177

stopped thinking about you and missing *us*. Not once." Gran waves the envelope in the air. "It's a voucher for a month long trip cruising around the world. How amazing is that?"

"Beats cooking lessons," Ethan says quietly, smiling.

"He'd better have his excuse for leaving rehearsed to the nth degree," Gran mutters. Putting the envelope back together, she slides it into the bag the way she found it. "Goodnight, you two." Waving, she turns toward the stairs.

I gape. "Where are you going?"

"To bed. I'm old. Who expects me to stay up past nine? I would tell you two to be good, but what's the fun in that?" Winking, she walks upstairs, a wicked cackle floating behind her.

"Your Gran is awesome." Ethan chuckles and clasps my hand. "Thanks for delivering."

"On what?"

Tugging me close, he drops a kiss on my nose. "A very entertaining evening."

"I'm glad *you* enjoyed it. My stomach's been tied in knots. Do you think Houdini is going to be okay? I would feel so awful if the mistletoe is what made him sick."

"Yeah, I'm pretty sure it's from overeating. Your dad didn't mention anything else when he went out, and I didn't sense any confusion in him, which I would have if he'd been poisoned."

I nod and tug him over to the couch. "Sit here. I'm going to get your present. It was too big to fit under the tree...or to wrap properly."

His eyes light up. "Too big, huh?"

"Close your eyes and don't open them until I tell you to, okay?"

He closes his eyes and murmurs, "What could possibly be too big to wrap?"

I go to the hall closet and get Ethan's gift, then lightly set it in his lap and say, "Okay." His hands intuitively grip the acoustic guitar before his eyes open. The look of love and appreciation he gives me is worth the money I spent on his gift. "I wanted a rosewood Martin for you, and a new one's a bit out of my price range. This one has only had one owner, so—"

"You always know how to knock me in the gut. It's perfect. Thank you, Nara," he says, quietly.

"I'm not done. I'm making up for missing your birthday." I retrieve his other gift from under the tree. Handing it to him, I grin. "This one, I could wrap."

Ethan leans the guitar against the couch, then tears off the wrapping paper. As he holds up the leather bound book with blank pages, I tap on the spine. "This book is only for drawings that make you happy. No demons or dark, nightmare images allowed. This is for ones to keep."

Ethan rubs his thumb along the spine, his gaze subdued and sincere. "Thank you for accepting every part of me, Sunshine."

"I love you, Ethan. Every glorious, beautiful side of you." Smiling, I run my fingertips along the strings on the guitar. "Maybe one day you can teach me how to play."

His fingers fold over mine on the guitar's neck, a playful look in his eyes. "How about a short lesson now?"

I don't even get to answer before he pulls me between his legs and lifts the guitar, settling it on my thighs.

After he fiddles with the strings, tuning them quietly for a minute, he folds my fingers, placing them on certain strings, then shows me how to strum. "Okay, now you do it by yourself."

I strum my finger down the strings and the soft sound floats around us.

"That's a G," he whispers in my ear. "Stands for, *God*, I love you more every day."

179

Goose bumps scatter across my skin when he switches my finger placement and tells me to strum the strings again. "That's a B, for *Be* Mine."

My heart races as his strong arms surround me to manipulate my fingers once more. Putting his hand over mine, we strum the next chord together. "And an F." He runs his nose along my neck until his mouth touches my ear. "That represents *Forever*, Sunshine."

When he kisses my cheek, my fingers grip the guitar, but as his mouth moves to my jaw, my heart melts and I whisper, "Together 'til the wheels fall off."

Ethan's arm cinches tight around my waist and he gently tugs my chin to press his mouth to mine. I don't even remember releasing the guitar, but Ethan turns me to gain better access to my mouth, pressing me deeper into the couch. I start to reach around his ribcage to pull him closer when my hand hits something wet.

I pull back. A smear of blood coats my palm. "Oh, God. Ethan you're hurt." He glances down when I tug his sweater up to inspect his wound. "That looks like a cut," I hiss angrily in a low voice, then push his shoulder so I can get up.

He clasps my hand. "I'll be fine, Nara. It'll be healed in a couple of days."

I frown and tug him to his feet. "You didn't say anything about being sliced up."

Ethan shrugs like it's no big deal, but he lets me tug him into the bathroom anyway.

I set the medical kit on the counter and mutter about having to replenish the supplies before Mom gets suspicious. Ethan shuts the bathroom door, then reaches behind his neck to tug his sweater off over his head.

It's hard not to stare at his ripped body in the mirror. He

drops his sweater on the closed toilet, his reflection grinning at me. "This is cozy."

"Switch places with me and put your hands on the counter," I say, refusing to be drawn in by his suggestive smile.

Ethan sighs and we side-shuffle in the small space until he's in front of the sink and I'm by the door.

Once he does as I ask, I can see the wound on his side much better. It's not as bad as I first thought. The scab that had started to form had broken and is oozing. Ethan's back muscles and biceps flex while I apply alcohol and an antibiotic salve, then tape a couple squares of gauze over his wound.

"All good?" he says, sounding like he's ready to be done.

I frown at him. "Stay put for a minute and let me see if there are others that you don't know about."

"You won't be happy until you've checked." Spreading his hands flat on the counter, he holds still so I can inspect.

I lean over and start scanning the left side of his back from his shoulder to his hip. A couple of bruises show under his skin, but nothing ominous looking. Sliding my focus across his lower back, past the sword's blade, my line of sight traces the muscles covering his ribs with serious scrutiny. I pause on a semi-round reddish spot with a wavy design. It looks familiar, and I touch his skin, trying to place the pattern.

Ethan flexes under my touch but doesn't move or lift his head. The realization hits me like a kick in the gut…Actually, like a kick delivered by a soccer shoe. That's the pattern my brain just placed. I close my eyes and try not to cry. It hurts so much to think about him being a constant target. To think of him being cut, kicked or beaten. I know this is his reality, but seeing the physical results really hits home and tears my heart in two. It's like his dreams have finally come to life. How freaking unfair is that?

Exhaling through my nose to calm my inner anger, I continue to slide my gaze up his back and my eyes stutter on the Corvus symbol at the top of his sword just under the handle. It's the raven yin-yang design I've seen many times, but this time something is different on the white raven's wing.

I hold my breath and step closer until my chest touches his back, then squint at the symbol because I think my eyes are playing tricks on me. But they're not.

"Oh, Ethan…" I whisper.

"What?" He jerks his head up, a cocky, devil-may-care smile on his face. "Another wound I didn't know about?"

I shake my head and stare at the one word written in a fancy script. "When did you get my name tattooed on the white raven?"

Ethan stills and a serious expression settles on his face. "You will always be my light, Nara. The other half of me." Vulnerability briefly flashes in his eyes. "Do you like it?"

It makes me sad that he sees himself as fully dark, but I adore that he sees me as his other half. "I love it," I say, then reach up and trace my fingers on my name along the white raven's wing.

Ethan drops his head and shudders, then groans out my name in a warning tone.

"What?"

His hands curl into fists on the counter. "You need to stop or I won't apologize for what happens between us in this shoebox of a bathroom."

"But I'm just touching one small part." I tease lightly, still surprised how much my touch on his tattoo affects him.

His head snaps up and his darkened gaze narrows,

locking with mine in the mirror. "You're lighting a match, Nara."

The full force of his burning stare sends heat roaring through me, making me want to see what happens when he loses even a tiny bit of control.

I bite my lip and slowly slide my finger down the black raven's wing this time.

CHAPTER 15

NARA

*B*efore my finger reaches the bottom of the black raven's wing, my back's against the door, and Ethan's chest is pressed to mine. Setting his hands flat against the door above my head, Ethan looks down at me, raw intensity shimmering in his eyes. "Last chance to call it quits."

His heart thumps hard against mine, making my pulse jump even more. I slide my arms around his neck and pull his mouth close to mine, whispering against his lips, "What fun is that?"

Ethan's mouth crushes mine, and I accept the hard press of his lips with fervor. His hands slide to my butt, gripping tight, and he steps between my legs, pressing his hardness intimately against me. Thrilled, I dig my fingers into his hair and swallow my moan of pleasure that rushes to the surface, keeping it locked inside where I can savor the vibration running through me. Tangling my tongue with his, I suck his bottom lip between mine, then slowly pull back, nipping his lip before I come back for more.

I feel the suppressed rumble in his chest a split second

before he breaks our kiss and grips the bottom of my sweater. He yanks it over my head in one swift movement, and I'm lifted in his arms before the sweater hits the floor. We fall against the door once more completely lost in each other.

Excitement zips through me, the heat between us burning hotter than it ever has before. I wrap my legs tight around his hips, then let out a quiet gasp of delight when he rolls his hips and a jolt of desire radiates from my center, splintering all the way to my toes and fingertips. I flatten my palms over his broad shoulders and start to slide them down his back, wanting to explore all of his warm skin.

"Don't touch my tattoo," he says in a low warning against my jaw.

"But you just let me. Twice."

"That's about all I can handle right now." He swallows and shakes his head, his body vibrating under me. "It's so freaking intense, Nara. I can't describe it. One day, I'll let you have at it and hope to hell I don't have a heart attack."

He sounds so on edge, I cup his face to calm him and whisper, "I love that you added my name to your tattoo. Does that make me a Corvus by proxy now?"

A quick laugh rumbles, and he dips his head to press his lips to the curve of my breast above my bra. When his eyes snap back to mine, blue and black swirl in the depths. "It makes you *everything* to me."

Emotion clogs my throat and I blink back tears, worrying what the future holds once he finally accepts that he's the Master Corvus. "You are my rock, my solid foundation, my home. No matter what happens, you always will be."

"Nothing is going to happen to me," he rasps against my jaw before nipping at my earlobe. His strong hands grip my hips and he settles my body right where he wants me.

Rocking into me, he moves slow and purposefully, setting a seductive pace.

My breathing elevates to the arousing rhythm building between us. "Promise?" I pant in his ear, my desire spiraling.

"I've come too far to lose the one thing in my life that matters by something as lame as dying."

I'm so on edge, I'm going to fly apart any second, but I need to hear him say everything will be okay. I fist a hand in his hair and tug slightly, hissing, *"Promise me, Ethan."*

"Damn, you jack me up." His fingers dig into my rear and he surges against me. Adding just the right amount of blissful pressure, he groans in my ear, "Cross my heart, Sunshine."

I grip him tight and cry out his name against his neck. Quivering all over, I absorb the waves of euphoria rolling through me. While my body trembles, Ethan murmurs his love along my jaw and we slide sideways, apparently hitting the light switch.

The tiny room douses in complete darkness, at least for a split second until our eyes adjust. Then a glowing light partially illuminates the room. Just when I vaguely wonder if Mom added a glowing Christmas plug-in to the bathroom, Ethan quickly sets me down, and the room goes dark once more.

"Did you see that?"

He sounds so freaked out, I start to reach for the light switch, but he says, "Don't turn on the light."

"Why?"

"Just wait."

We stand there in the bathroom, breathing heavily for a couple of seconds. Finally I say, "Are you going to tell me what's going on?"

"I think it'd be better if I showed you."

"Okaaaay." Why is he acting so weird? "Wouldn't that be easier with the light on?"

"Move in front of me," he says, sounding calmer, assured.

"I am in front of you."

"No, stand in front of me facing the mirror."

I move in front of him. "What am I supposed to see in the dark?"

"Watch," he says right before he folds his hand over my right shoulder.

"What are you seeing that I can't?"

"Hmm, something else must cause it..." he mumbles right before his other hand slides down my belly. The second his fingers brush the waistband on my jeans, a low glow lights up around his hand.

"What the—?" I gasp just as Ethan removes his hand and the room goes dark once more.

"I think I know what the trigger is now," he says next to my ear, his voice confident and seductive. Fingertips trail down my cleavage next, and a burst of warm, glowing light follows their path. Once he moves his hand away, faint fingerprints glow on my skin. "When our touch is intimate, this warm illumination happens."

"This is crazy. It wasn't like this before. Why now?" I say, and Ethan quickly turns me to face him.

"Is it crazy?" he asks in the darkness. "We've grown closer, our love is stronger. Maybe it's just..." He slides his hand under my hair, cupping the back of my neck. When he traces his thumb along my jaw, a low light shines against our faces. It remains lit when he reaches my mouth and slides his thumb sensually along my bottom lip. "Us," he finishes simply, then presses his lips to mine.

I kiss him back, loving this unexpected uniqueness happening between us. Ethan never ceases to amaze me. His charisma is so addicting, he's like a drug I just can't get enough of. This new layer only enhances our intimacy. I touch his jaw, expecting glowing warmth to spread under my fingertips. I laugh when nothing happens. "Hmmm, apparently you don't feel anything when I touch you."

"It's indescribable what I feel when you touch me," he says in a low tone. "The word intimacy doesn't even begin to define it. The glow aspect must be a 'me to you' thing." A wicked smile flashes. "It'll make it easier for me to see which parts of you I haven't touched yet. You'll be lit up like a Christmas tree by the time I'm done with you."

The thought warms my cheeks, but then they flame when another realization flashes. How long does it last? And will others be able to see? I glance down to make sure my skin he already touched isn't still glowing. Thankfully, the effect has already faded.

Ethan chuckles. "Had you going there for a sec, didn't I?"

I smack his shoulder. "Not funny. Can you imagine my father's reaction if he saw your glowing handprints all over me?"

He wraps his arms around my waist and pulls me close. "I like this idea of branding your body from head to toe with my handprints. Sounds like an awesome plan."

"I think the feather on my shoulder will have to do." Giggling, I snake my arm around his waist and glide my other hand down the front of his jeans. "Now, where did we leave off?"

Grinning, he presses his aroused body against my palm. "You were about to show me—"

The sound of my cell phone ringing loudly jars us both into motion. I quickly open the door, then shrug into my sweater, and rush into the kitchen to grab the phone off the counter. The last thing I want is to wake Gran up.

"Hey, Mom. How's Houdini?"

"He's in with the vet now. The doctor thinks your Gran was right and Houdini just ate too much. But just to be safe he's running some tests."

"I'm glad the vet thinks Houdini's going to be okay."

Ethan joins me in the kitchen while my mom continues. "We're having some coffee across the street while we wait for the test results."

"Something is actually open?"

"Just a twenty-four-seven convenience store with a couple of booths. I imagine it'll be an hour or so before we get back. It was really tough getting here. The roads are a mess and the storm isn't letting up."

"Please drive safe...and I hope you enjoy your coffee."

"I will. I'm sorry this Christmas turned into such a disaster." Mom sighs heavily. "But on the bright side, I might have outgrown my allergies. I haven't sneezed once and Houdini has been laying all over me."

At least my Mom found something positive about the evening. "Does this mean I won't have to vacuum twice a week now?"

"Don't even try to wiggle out of that chore, young lady. Got to go. Your father just brought our coffees."

I want to beg her to listen if dad tries to talk to her about the past, but they seem to have struck a kind of truce for now, so I don't bring it up. "Okay, see you soon."

After I hang up, Ethan sets a jewelry box with a red bow on the counter. "My turn to give you your gift. Merry Christmas."

I open the velvet lid and gasp in happiness. "It's beautiful." Holding the ID-style bracelet up to inspect the single angel wing, I smile when the light catches on the diamond cuts on the wing's unique cutout design. It's similar to filigree, but the pattern is more symmetrically angular than the twisted curls and loops I've seen in most filigree work.

Ethan takes the bracelet from me and lays the inch long wing across my wrist, then hooks the bracelet's delicate chain. Lifting my arm, he presses a kiss to the underside of my wrist next to the clasp. "I haven't been able to get that picture of you standing outside the hospital with snow in your hair out of my head. Even while you were giving me hell, you looked like an angel."

I smile at his comment, then glance down at the bracelet. "Thank you for the beautiful gift. The wing has an unusual cutout pattern."

Ethan nods. "It does."

Threading my fingers with his, I turn off the kitchen light, then pull him into the living room where I turn off the lamps until the only light in the room is the colorful lights on the Christmas tree.

"I want to share something with you that I used to do as a kid. You ready?"

He kisses my knuckles. "Sure."

I release his hand, then get down on my hands and knees to push some of the presents under the tree out of the way.

"What are you doing?" he asks, clearly baffled.

I glance at him over my shoulder. "Just help me move some of these."

He gets down beside me and helps.

Once the presents are cleared, I smile at him. "Follow my lead." Laying down on my back, I slide under the tree until my head and shoulders are under the branches.

Ethan joins me. Shoulder bumping me lightly, he lets out a low chuckle. "This isn't at all what I expected. Now what?"

I clasp his hand and turn my head until I'm looking up through the branches. "When I was little, I used to lay under the Christmas tree and stare up through the branches to all the shiny bulbs, crystals, and twinkling lights and make a wish."

Ethan's hand squeezes mine and sincerity replaces the amusement in his tone. "What did you wish for, Nara? What was your heart's desire when you were little?"

A tear trickles down my temple. "I wished for my dad to return." Sniffing my emotions back, I turn my head to look at him. "What was your heart's desire when you were little?"

"I wished for a guardian angel to watch over me so I could be as bad as I wanted to be but would always be safe."

"Really?" I laugh. I can't help it. "You were quite the little hellion, weren't you?"

Ethan flashes a mischievous grin. "Looks like we both got what we wished for. Your dad is back in your life and I got a guardian angel."

I shake my head. "Dad is here, but not with my mom."

"I'd like to point out that the mistletoe did its job. Just not in the way we expected it to. Your parents are together right now. Don't lose hope yet."

"I'm not holding my breath. And I would hardly call Michael your guardian angel. He has let so much happen to you, and sadly, you can't even talk to him."

"I wasn't talking about Michael." Ethan lifts our clasped hands under the tree between us and slides the bracelet around on my wrist. "Whether you're from the Celestial realm or not, Nara, you ground me and give me peace." Touching the wing, he slides his finger across the shiny cutout design. "I'll answer your question about snowflakes now. The one attribute snowflakes have over rain is their footprint. Each snowflake's pattern is entirely unique. That's what you are to me. My very own, unique angel."

I stare at the angel wing. That's what the unusual design was inside the wing. The jeweler had taken a snowflake pattern and then bent and morphed the edges into the shape of an angel's wing. My heart just melted a little bit more, falling even deeper in love with him.

"Thank you for the thoughtful gift." I roll onto my side and scootch closer to him. Resting my head on his shoulder, I slide my hand up his shirt and trace my fingertips along his abs. "But the last thing I feel like at the moment is angelic."

Ethan can't roll over under the tree like me; his shoulders are too broad, so he clasps the back of my thigh and pulls my leg over his, locking me tight against him. "I think you're perfect just the way you are."

"Ever made out under a Christmas tree?" I say. "We'll have to keep it PG-13 but—"

Ethan presses his mouth hard to mine for a second, then follows with a tender kiss, murmuring against my lips, "I can't think of a better place to create some new wishes. Tell me your heart's desire, Sunshine."

CHAPTER 16

NARA

I walk to the edge of the woods, my snow boots clomping through the deep snow. A crisp breeze blows through the trees, drawing my gaze to the ripples rolling across the water in the icy pond. It's our place.

Ethan's and mine.

Where is he?

I scan the open field around the pond, but don't see Ethan anywhere.

The wind blows again, lifting my hair and freezing the tips of my ears. I shudder and start to zip my jacket, but I'm not wearing one, so I wrap my arms around my body and shiver to stay warm while I move closer to the pond.

The water is perfectly still now that the breeze has stopped. Panic grips my chest as I stare at the frozen chunks of ice floating in the water. They seem larger than they were before. What if Ethan is under there and I don't know it?

"Ethan!" I scream, terror shooting sharp pains in my stomach.

Nothing.

I call his name several more times, but all I hear is my own fear echoing back at me through the woods.

A group of ravens take off from the top of a tree. I track their movement and want to call after them, to beg them to tell me where Ethan is, but they're gone before I can utter a word.

Wrapping my arms tight around my churning stomach, I continue to stare at the pond until my eyes burn. What if Ethan's stuck under one of the big pieces of ice? Something moves in my periphery, and when I look up, Ethan's standing a few feet away, watching me with a furrowed brow.

"You're here!" I smile happily and stomp through the thick snow toward him. "I'm so relieved. I was worried you were in the water."

He doesn't speak. He just smirks and puts his hand out. I slip mine inside of his. As I walk along beside him, soaking up his warmth, I wonder about his subdued mood. He seems deep in thought.

He leads me along the edge of the pond, and before I can blink, my perspective changes. I shriek when I suddenly land on a thick branch high up in a massive tree. I grip a limb above my head, my whole body shaking from the fast change in location. Once I get my bearings and can breathe normally again, I peer around us. It's surreal being up so high. We're higher than most of the treetops, creating the illusion that I can see forever. We must be in the white oak tree. I smile at the clumps of mistletoe on branches just a few feet above us.

Ethan follows my line of sight. "Could've gotten that mistletoe down much easier if I'd wanted to." While he quickly lowers himself onto the thick limb, his movements assured and graceful, his actions remind me of Drystan's prowess and confidence on the bouncy, one-inch slackline.

Once he leans back against the tree's trunk, Ethan holds a hand up for me to join him. I grip his hand tight and take a much longer time letting go of the limb above my head to finally lower myself to his level. Heart racing, I let him hold both my hands while I squat and turn on the limb. As soon as I straddle the thick branch like him, he pulls me back against his chest.

We sit there, staring out over the treetops. He hasn't spoken for at least a half hour, so I just let him be at peace with his own thoughts. Something is definitely on his mind.

After a few more minutes pass, he puts his hand out in front of me, palm up. I lay my palm flat on top of his and he lowers our hands to his thigh.

"I'm not Ethan," he finally says in a voice I've only heard a few times before; it's older and wiser, like Michael's.

"I'm dreaming right now, aren't I?" I say, lifting my palm off his and sitting up. I knew something felt off about Ethan. The superior arrogance alone should've clued me in. I'm surprised by how calm I am, but I know the Corvus would never hurt me.

When he stiffens, then answers, "Yes," I realize this is a perfect opportunity to get inside the spirit's head and find out what happened in the past. But first I want to know who he is. If I learn more about him, it might help me better deal with Ethan when his Corvus affects his moods. I turn to look at him. "What should I call you?"

"I'm Corvus."

I roll my eyes. "That's your designation, your...species, not your name."

He frowns. "Why do I need a name?"

"So I don't address you as, 'hey you.'"

"You're looking at me. Of course, you're talking to me."

His logic is so literal and laced with stubbornness, it's hard not to laugh, but I manage. "Have it your way." I sigh and turn back around. "Do you know who you are?" I ask the winter-bare tree branches.

He cups my jaw, turning me to face him once more. "I don't have a name."

I smile inwardly. He's thawing some. "How about Rave?"

He stares at me blankly, then appears to roll the name around in his head. "I suppose Rave works."

"Do you know what you are, Rave?"

Pride flashes in his eyes. "I'm Corvus," he says once more like that explains everything.

"No, you're more than that. You're special."

Arrogance stamps his features. "All Corvus are special."

I start to shake my head, to clarify, but he captures my chin between his knuckle and thumb, halting my movement. "You are unique."

I snort. That's the last thing I expected to hear. "Yeah, I'm a lightweight, remember? That's pretty dang unique."

Amusement shows on his face for the first time. He likes that I remember him calling me that in an earlier dream. "Your lightness is a gift, part of your nature. It's incredibly rare."

"I'm confused. Why is lightness rare?"

"I just know it's fleeting."

Is he remembering something from his past? "How do you know it's fleeting?"

Rave shrugs and glances away. "Because darkness is my world."

I tap his shoulder, and he returns his dark eyes to mine. "Does it have to be? Why can't you have some light in your world too?"

A flash of surprise glimmers in his dark eyes. Then uncertainty. Finally he stiffens. "There is no choice."

"There can be for you. You have the power to change it.

You just have to accept who you are. You're not one of many, Rave. You're one of a kind. You're the Master—"

He jerks his head back and forth, saying forcefully, "No, I'm just Corvus. Nothing more."

Before I can say anything else, he leans sideways and then pitches straight down off the branch. His swift retreat jars the limb, and I grip the thick branch underneath me to keep from falling. Just when I call his name, he shifts to a massive raven and shreds through his clothes, growing to the size of a car. Swooping close to the pond, he pulls water with him as he flaps his powerful wings once, twice. The third time sends him soaring high above the trees and out of my line of sight in a matter of seconds.

The look of angry defiance on his face struck me. He doesn't want to believe or accept what I say. When I tried to tell him what he was, he shut me out. Frustration rolls through me and I dig my fingers into the branch's rough bark. How am I going to convince a supernatural being that he possesses massive power and has duties and responsibilities when all he wants to do is refuse them?

"Well, damn," I whisper when the irony hits me. I can't believe that Michael has tasked me with a role not unlike Fate's. The only difference is, whereas Fate wanted to quash my powers, the Master Corvus is refusing to accept all of his. This path-leading job isn't easy. I'm just glad Fate can't hear my thoughts. He'd be laughing his ass off and quoting karma sayings right now. I clench my jaw at the mere thought.

Nara, you there? Drystan's voice filters into my frustrated thoughts.

How is he in my dream world? I whip my head around, looking for him, when a tree branch brushes against my cheek.

CHAPTER 17

NARA

I jerk awake to the sensation of something prickly brushing my face. Christmas bulbs tinkle against each other and colorful lights' reflections bounce off the furniture as my head jostles some of the tree branches.

"What is it?" Ethan says groggily.

"Shhh." I press my finger to his lips and rest my chin on his chest, closing my eyes.

—*you there?* Drystan's voice bleeds back in. *Ah, there you are. Wow, I feel you now. My brain just lit up. I was beginning to think our connection was just a one time fluke. Damn, this rocks.*

I didn't find your book in the library where the computer system said it would be. Another was in its spot, some touristy book on London. I'm not sure if that's good news or not, but now you know for sure. There's not a second book. Merry Christmas, Nara. I'm off to some tree-lighting Christmas event the whole sanctuary is required to attend.

When I sigh my frustration and open my eyes, Ethan pushes my hair back from my face. "What's wrong?"

"Drystan checked the library for me. Another book has apparently been put in the place of the raven book."

Ethan frowns warily. "When did Drystan tell you this?"

"Um." I hadn't told him about the odd connection Drystan and I have. I thought I'd wait for Drystan to contact me this way on purpose first. "Just now."

He tenses under me. "Are you saying you just had a whole conversation telepathically?"

My stomach knots when several emotions scroll across his face. None of them happy. I shake my head. "I can't talk to him. I just hear what he's saying."

"How long has this been happening?" he asks, only the sound of the front door opening interrupts us. Before I can move, Houdini comes barreling toward me covered in snow.

"Hey, buddy," I say, rubbing his head as he licks me on the cheek. "Looks like you're back to your old self again."

"What are you still doing here?" My dad says while Ethan leans over to help me to my feet.

"We fell asleep under the tree," I say, gesturing to the spot where we'd pushed presents to the side.

"This is what I was talking to you about, Elizabeth." My father's attention snaps to my mom, who's looking bone tired as she hooks her coat and scarf on the rack.

Suddenly my mom's shoulders straighten. "That's enough, Jonathan. It's Christmas, and this is *my* home."

Turning to Ethan, she says, "Your car is completely covered. You won't be getting it out tonight."

"I can walk home, Mrs. Collins. It's not that far—"

"Absolutely not," Mom cuts in. "The temperature has dropped to the single digits. You can sleep here on the floor. Just send your brother a text so he doesn't worry about you."

Facing my dad, she says, "I doubt you'll get a taxi this late. I'm pretty sure everyone's hunkered in for the night. You're welcome to the couch. I'm going to bed." Waving to us, she starts up the stairs and calls over her shoulder,

"Nara, get our guests some blankets and pillows. Jonathan will cook pancakes tomorrow morning in payment for staying the night."

"I will?" my dad asks, surprised sarcasm lacing his tone.

When my mom stops on the stairs, but doesn't turn around, he immediately says, "Pancakes it is. Night, Elizabeth."

She doesn't say another word, just continues up to the second floor.

I'm a nervous wreck when I come back downstairs with blankets and pillows for my dad and Ethan. I already gave them new toothbrushes—for some odd reason Mom always keeps a fresh supply of toothbrushes handy.

I poke my head in the open bathroom doorway just as my dad's spitting toothpaste foam into the sink. "I'll put your pillow and blanket on the couch, Dad." Then I lower my voice just for him and say in a forceful tone, "Be nice to him."

He grunts and sets the toothbrush down, saying, "Good-night, Nari," before he turns and closes the door to finish up his nightly routine.

I hand Ethan his pillow and blankets, and grimace. "I'm going to apologize now if my dad gives you a hard time tonight."

"There's nothing your dad can say to me that would be any worse than what I've heard from my own dad," Ethan says, gathering the covers under his arm.

"I know you would've been fine walking in that crazy weather out there, so thank you for staying for my mom's sake. She would've worried you would freeze to death on your way home."

He kisses me on the forehead, but when he straightens, he has the same look on his face he did earlier. "About Drystan—"

My dad opens the bathroom door, cutting off our conversation. I give Ethan an apologetic smile, then wave goodnight.

By the time I wash my face and crawl into bed, I have two texts from Ethan.

Ethan: Is the Drystan thing recent?

Ethan: I'm not freaking out. Just wondering.

Me: It seems a little like you're freaking out. Ever since Drystan arrived in England, if he thinks my name, I hear his thoughts. After all my attempts to contact Madeline failed, I got worried someone might already be after the second book, so I asked Drystan to check the library for me. He thought it'd be faster to 'think' the answer to me.

Ethan: Did something happen to Madeline?

Me: Her website is gone. Her email bounces. None of my earlier contact information with her works. It's like she never existed.

Ethan: Hopefully Madeline's fine. As for Drystan, I know how he feels about you, Nara. I don't want him in your head.

Drystan's not the only one in my head. But I can't say anything to Ethan about what I heard that day in his car. I'm still not sure if I imagined it, since it just happened the one time.

Me: He was only helping me out.

Ethan: I know. There's something else I want to talk to you about tomorrow. Then I think you'll understand why I'm feeling the way I do.

Me: How are you feeling?

Ethan: Territorial.

That's an interesting word choice. Very Corvus of him. I type an answer back that should help.

Me: TTTWFO

Ethan: I love you, Sunshine. Night.

Me: Love you too. Night.

ETHAN

NARA'S DAD never said a word to me, but like a guard dog ready to strike if I moved a muscle, he kept his distrustful gaze on my back for at least an hour before he finally succumbed to sleep. Now that his breathing has evened out, I roll onto my back and stare at the ceiling in the darkness.

The conversation I had earlier with the Corvus plays through my head in an endless, frustrating loop, keeping me wide awake.

Nara's head hitting the tree woke me, but when she asked me to be quiet and confusion rolled through me, that's when the Corvus piped in.

Drystan's in her head.

My gut tightened. Was this some new form of torture he has decided to inflict on me now? *She's not thinking about him.*

I didn't say that. He's talking to her. At least he was in her dream.

My hand resting on Nara's back curled into a fist. *How do you know that?*

Because I was there.

It took massive effort to remain still under Nara when all I wanted to do was punch the stupid spirit. *Why?*

I told you...her lightness is addicting.

My heart constricted with worry. I had been right to yank my hand away from her face last night after I saved her from that demon. It wasn't me touching her. *And I told you to stay the hell away from her.*

This again? You have to keep your distance for that to happen, and we both know you can't.

His egotistical confidence set me off. *Screw you, Corvus!*

You may call me Rave.

He sounded like a prince bestowing me with his permission. *Hop off, you self-important feather-covered rat. Rave? Really?* I mentally snorted.

That's my name.

Since when?

I like it. It's—

Dumb, I said in a droll tone.

—self-explanatory.

Corny.

I don't think Nara's dumb or corny. Should I tell her you do? He laughed heartily at that.

The fact that he sounded pleased with his new name ticked me off even more. *She named you like a pet, same way she did Patch,* I gritted out.

I am not *an animal. I am beyond your comprehension!* The Corvus roared so loud it felt like my brain was vibrating in my skull. And then he was gone. Nara sighing her frustration yanked me out of my own head. Lying on the floor under the tree with her felt so peaceful, I didn't want it to end. I brushed her hair out of her face just so I could touch her and asked what was wrong.

A clock ticking quietly somewhere in Nara's living room brings me back to the present. The repetitiveness sounds fast, but it's taking forever. The morning can't get here soon enough. I really don't like the idea of Drystan being able to pop into her head whenever he wants, but right now I'm more worried about the Corvus.

I fold my arms behind my head and try to figure out the Corvus' angle. What does he want? Did he talk to Nara just to freak me out? Or is there more to it?

A sudden flash of memory ricochets around in my skull and the pain is so fierce I grip my head. When the aching stops, and I'm finally able to unclench my jaw, a sheen of sweat coats my entire body. Blowing out a quiet breath, I fist my hands in my hair and whisper, "Fucking hell."

~

NARA

FORTY MINUTES before sunrise I crouch beside Ethan and hold my steaming mug of coffee close to his nose. When his eyes fly open and he starts to say something, I quickly press my finger to his lips and shake my head. I glance at my dad, who's snoring lightly on the couch, then lift my finger and curl it toward me as I stand.

Ethan follows me up the stairs, and then sits facing me once we reach a place—three steps from the top—where the stairwell wall comes down and will block us from my dad's view.

Ethan looks so devastatingly handsome, with mussed hair and an overnight beard on his jaw, I set my phone on the stairs and twine my yoga-panted legs with his jean-covered ones, just to be close to him. Leaning toward him, I say in a quiet voice, "Merry Christmas. I didn't make you a cup of coffee since you claim not to like it."

Ethan tucks a strand of my hair behind my ear, his act so tender I want to kiss him. "If it only tasted as good as it smelled, I'm sure I'd love it."

I hug the cup between my hands and take a sip, letting its warmth chase the morning chill away. "I thought you might like to talk before everyone gets up."

Nodding, he reaches for one of my hands and turns me around on the stairs until my body's tucked between his legs. "This is much better," he says in a husky tone, bending down to kiss me on the cheek.

I lean fully into his hard chest and the warm circle of his arms, snuggling close. "I agree."

Just when I start to take another sip of my coffee, he steals the cup and swallows a big gulp, then hands it back to me. "Hmmm, Nara-coffee tastes like manna from heaven."

My stomach flutters. He always finds a way to make me feel special. Holding the warm cup with both hands once more, I glance up at him. "Tell me what's bothering you."

He's quiet for a second, like he's choosing his words carefully, then he says, "The Corvus told me Drystan was in your head while he was talking to you about the library. He heard Drystan in your dream."

My eyes widen. "Your Corvus is talking to you now?" I'm not sure if this is a good thing or a bad thing. "What did he say?"

Ethan frowns down at me. "That you named him Rave."

"Oh, that." My face flames, and I shrug. "I thought giving him a name might help him open up."

"He doesn't need to open up," Ethan grates. "I don't like the idea of anyone talking to you in your head, Nara. Not Drystan, nor that stupid bird, spirit…whatever the hell it is."

"So this is where that 'territorial' comment came from last night."

He scowls. "It's not because I'm jealous."

I raise my eyebrows. "Oh, really?"

Shrugging, he grunts. "I guess that's part of it, but I'm more worried about how having someone in your head can affect and influence you. Trust me, I know what I'm talking about."

"If you know what you're talking about—I'm assuming you mean your Corvus—then you also know that you can still stay true to yourself no matter how strong the mental influence. You did."

He opens his mouth like he's going to say something

else, then closes it. A muscle jumps along his jawline for a few seconds. Then he finally speaks. "I believe you now."

"Believe me about what?"

"That I'm the Master Corvus."

Relief flows through me and I turn sideways, hooking my elbow around his thigh. "That's good news. Things will be so much easier now that the Master Corvus is back on track—why are you shaking your head?"

Ethan points to his chest. "I said, *I* now believe that I'm carrying around the Master Corvus. The spirit hasn't accepted that truth about himself yet."

"Oh." My shoulders slump, and I drop my chin on his bent knee. "He's very stubborn." Tilting my head slightly, I glance back at him, curious what changed. "What made you finally accept what I've been telling you?"

Ethan runs his hand from the top of my head to the ends of my hair, then he traces his finger along my slouchy sweatshirt's collar. "This."

I glance down as he tugs the sweatshirt off my shoulder to reveal the feather tattoo on my shoulder blade. "My feather?"

But Ethan's gaze snaps to mine, his brow furrowed. "When did it turn white again?"

"It did?" I crane to see the tattoo, then give up. I can only see it in the mirror. "I have no idea. And what does the Master Corvus have to do with it?"

Ethan shakes his head, a mystified look on his face as he slides his fingers across my tattoo. "He's the only one who can see it, Nara."

"What?" I turn to face him so fast I almost spill my coffee. "What do you mean? I see it just fine and so do you. Also, pretty important question. How do you know that you're the Master Corvus, yet he doesn't?"

Ethan shrugs. "I know things he doesn't because part of

my thoughts are sectioned off from him. I don't know how it works, but it just does. He hates that my mind is strong enough that I can keep some things from him if I want to. For once the tables are turned though. I apparently got a flash of one of his memories last night."

My heart pounds double time. "What did you see?"

"It's not what I saw, it's more like information came through." His fingers trace my tattoo. "This is how the angels mark those worthy of being Corvus, Nara. It's invisible to everyone but the Master Corvus. Once the Master Corvus chooses who to give a part of himself to, a feather surfaces as an outline on the new Corvus' shoulder blade, then it changes to a black feather—"

"Before morphing into a sword," I finish for him. "I know I'm not Corvus, and apparently you aren't responsible for this feather on my shoulder, so why is it visible?"

Ethan slides his thumb down my tattoo, a possessive look reflected in his eyes. "We weren't wrong in our assumption about your tattoo, Nara. When we connected in that coach's closet and I wished with all my heart to claim you as mine, the Corvus heard my thoughts." His blue eyes snap to mine. "Your feather would only have risen to the surface if he claimed you, but he didn't give you a part of his Corvus self."

I swallow and grip the coffee cup tight. "What does that mean? Was he claiming me for you then?"

Ethan sets his mouth in a grim line. "I doubt he was being charitable to me. It would be a first. That's the extent of what I got from the memory. It was enough to tell me for sure that he's the Master Corvus, but not why he raised your feather."

I might not know why I have it, but since the feather surfaced because of the Master Corvus…. "Maybe that's why I knew where all the Corvus are in the world. It was never me. It was the feather."

Ethan leans back against the railing and sighs. "If he didn't give you a part of himself, then how can that be?"

He has a point. I chew my lip and ponder. As we sit there in silence, lost in our thoughts, the rising sun slowly snakes its rays through the banister and up the stairwell. The beams hit the lights on the Christmas tree just right, reflecting blue, red, teal, and purple colors along the wall across from us.

"Look, a Christmas rainbow," I say quietly, pointing to the spray of color.

As Ethan nods, our heat kicks on and some of the tree limbs move with the vent pushing warm air up through them. The colors on the wall bounce and jostle around. When I see the red color juddering back and forth on top of the purple, the two colors together make me think about the map Ethan and I burned.

I grab Ethan's thigh and squeeze. "I just had an idea. I think I might know what I was supposed to see on that map with the purple and red marks."

"You do? What?"

"Well, remember that the purple marks I put on the map represented areas around the world where unusual phenomena had happened not long after a natural disaster event had occurred—which we know might have been possible tears in the veil. And the red dots that my *feather* plotted on the map are supposed to be the Corvus all over the world, right?"

He nods. "So how are they connected?"

"What if, by putting these two together, we could possibly create a resource of information to help the Corvus narrow down an area where a possible Inferi might take over a human?"

Ethan looks intrigued. "So instead of hunting a wide

range and hoping to run across a human inhabited by a demon, now a Corvus could be more proactive and precise in how he or she hunts?"

"Exactly. It would take computer resources or a group of dedicated people to track events and such like I did…" I pause while my brain flies through the possibilities of this new technique. "All the data crunching could possibly be centralized at the Order—I know they have computer skills, since they tracked me through mine. Then the Order could send out alerts for potential demon activity in specific areas for the Corvus to keep under surveillance." I grin in my excitement. "It's not foolproof, but something like this could cut down on the amount of time demons can hide inside people before they're discovered by a Corvus."

When I take a breath, Ethan's eyes are shining with pride. "That's just brilliant, Nara! Why has no one else thought of this?"

I spread my hands wide. "I only thought of it because I saw the veil tearing. Seeing that happen more than once, and then talking to Madeline about what causes the veil to thin, made me wonder about the correlation. I didn't know what to do with the information I had compiled until just now."

"You are truly amazing," Ethan says, shaking his head. "Though I'd like you to wait and see what Drystan thinks about the Order before you present this idea to them."

"So you trust Drystan's opinion now?"

He snorts. "No, but I believe he wouldn't let you be involved with something untrustworthy. And the fact that he's not pro-Order right now works in his favor as far as I'm concerned."

When I start to question why he thinks I should wait, he holds up a finger. "Once Drystan gives a thumbs up about the Order and you decide to present this idea to them, you must insist that the potential breakthrough information only be provided to the Corvus manually, not electronically."

"Why not? Electronic is faster and more efficient."

"For the same reason we had to destroy the map; demons would love to find out where every Corvus lives. Any electronic information leaving the Order can be traced. My suggestion would be to add messenger duties to the Paladin's current ones with the Corvus. I'm pretty sure the Paladins would agree. I doubt I'm wrong in assuming they're honor bound to keep their Corvus' locations secret."

"Ah, good point. I wouldn't have thought of that part. Only a Corvus can think like a Corvus."

Ethan grins. "We're definitely better together, Sunshine."

I smile back. "And now that you have an inside track into the Master Corvus' mind, maybe together we can convince him who he really is and help him remember what happened."

"Actually, I think it's going to be even harder to convince him now," he says, rubbing the back of his neck.

"Why?"

He slowly twists a strand of my hair around his finger. "Because, like me, he doesn't want to let you go. He thinks he can protect you better than I can. I'm worried what he might do."

"He's spirit. What can he do?"

Ethan grips my waist and slides me closer to kiss my cheekbone. "While I still had amnesia I understood exactly what it felt like to walk around with power surging through me that I didn't understand or know how to control," he says in a low voice. "The Master Corvus is dangerous in his own invincibility. In his blind arrogance, he puts others at risk."

Ethan's somber mood worries me. I turn and meet his

gaze. "What has your Corvus done that you aren't telling me?"

"Nothing yet. It's what he could do without knowing the extent of his strength and power that I care about."

I start to ask Ethan more about his relationship with the Corvus when my dad grabs the banister at the bottom of the stairs, then starts up the staircase at a brisk pace, an angry, determined look on his face.

He stops halfway up the stairs when he sees us.

"Merry Christmas, Dad. Where are you going in such a hurry?" I say, then take a sip of my coffee to keep from smiling. I knew he thought Ethan was upstairs with me and was racing to catch us together.

"I uh..." He rubs his hand through his dark, messy bedhead hair. "I thought the bathroom was occupied downstairs."

I lean over to peer around him. "Nope, bathroom's all clear. Oh, the pancake mix is in the far right cabinet when you're ready to make them."

My dad looks from Ethan to me, then nods curtly and turns back down the stairs. When he shuts the bathroom door and we hear the faucet running, Ethan chuckles quietly.

"What?" I look at him innocently.

"You have a bit of a devilish streak." Tapping the end of my nose, he leans close and whispers in my ear, sounding captivated, "An angel with horns. Now that's hot. I love seeing this side of you."

Even though I grin, pleased by his comment, I feel like there's something he hasn't told me about his Corvus. I don't like to think of Ethan and the powerful spirit inside him not getting along. The next chance I get, I'll talk to the raven spirit about Ethan.

～

AN HOUR LATER, I pace by my front window and watch Ethan flinging snow with the shovel. After clearing a path for Houdini to do his business, he's now digging his car out. According to the news, it had snowed four feet in twenty-four hours. A new record for Blue Ridge. I stop pacing and gnaw the inside of my cheek, wanting to help. Ethan refused to let me, saying I should stay inside where it was warm. Sometimes he takes the whole "Southern gentleman" thing to extremes.

There's just too much snow for one person. I grimace, hating that he's out there by himself. Just as I move to grab my coat, my father says, "Come take your phone, Nari. It almost got swept into the trash with the egg carton."

Once I pick my phone up, Dad stops stirring the pancake batter and looks at me across the island. "I know something more is going on with that boy, Nara. Tell me what it is."

"Nothing, Dad."

My dad shakes his head. "That raven symbol means something. I'm not sure what, but something."

I curl my hand around my phone and mentally count to five so my voice sounds calm when I answer. "It really is a symbol of protection and good luck. Stop being so negative about Ethan. If you want to be a part of my life, I'd like you to try to accept him, because he's here to stay. Nothing you can say or do will change that."

CHAPTER 18

NARA

*A*fter taking Houdini out, I walk inside shivering at the brisk night air. Shrugging out of my coat, I hang it on the rack, glad that it had warmed up enough over the last few days to melt all the snow we'd gotten on Christmas Eve.

Mom has been working like crazy this past week to tie up some loose ends at work. I didn't say anything when she headed out during her "vacation time" this morning, calling behind her, "I'll be late, sweetie." I know what she's doing. I learned my avoidance techniques from her.

The day after Christmas, David called and made another excuse as to why he couldn't come over. Since then, he hasn't come by or called, which made it pretty clear to Mom that whatever they had was over. I'm sure she wonders if the reason he changed his mind about their relationship is because she invited my dad to dinner.

I feel bad that I'm partially to blame for chasing my mom's boyfriend off, but I console myself with the belief that if he could so easily dump my mom, then he's not worth her time.

Sighing, I give Houdini a dog biscuit, then pat him on the head. "It's just you and me tonight, buddy. Want to watch a movie?"

A text from my mom buzzes on my phone. When I check it, I see Ethan had sent me one while I was outside.

Mom: I think I'm ready to see those videos your father left you. Tomorrow night? We'll order pizza.

I smile at her text. Dad never did give Mom the Christmas present he brought for her. Maybe he realized it was too soon, but he has stayed in touch. He's been working out of Aunt Sage's house, and last night he called to tell me he'll be moving to Blue Ridge permanently in a couple weeks.

Me: Sounds good. Don't work too late.

Mom: Unfortunately all the work I've created this week means I have to stay to finish it. Bleh. Off to get it done.

I snicker, then read Ethan's text.

Ethan: Trying one more time with our parents. This restaurant is a hole in the wall that my Dad picked. He's usually the caviar type. Samson's skeptical. I'm either really hungry or pleasantly hopeful. What have you done to me?

I laugh, happy that they're trying again so soon.

Me: I make you smile.

Ethan: Always.

Feeling all warm inside, I start to set my phone down when it rings. I quickly answer it, smiling. "Hey Gran. Are you glad to be back in your own place now?"

"Hello, Inara, dear. I think you should come over. I need an intervention. I'm about to kill Clara."

Chuckling, I sit on the stool and tuck the phone between my shoulder and ear while I untie my shoe, then toe it off. "What new rivalry is going on between you two now? It's probably something I can handle over the phone with you."

"You're not hearing me, Nara. I need you to come now."

I freeze in toeing off my other shoe. Gran has never called me Nara. Nor has she ever spoken to me that way.

"Is everything okay, Gran? I mean *really* okay?"

"I want that book." Gran's voice had changed, sounding harsher. My face prickles as the demon continues, "You need to bring me the book or I'm going to kill the old woman. You have twenty minutes. Better hurry. The clock is ticking."

The demon hangs up, cutting off my chance to threaten him if anything happens to Gran.

My hands are shaking so bad, it takes me three tries to finally hit the button to dial Ethan's number. While it rings, I clamp my lips shut to keep from panting and jam my foot back into my tennis shoe.

"Nara?"

"I know you can't talk. Just listen," I gush out. "Harper's Inferi has Gran. I have to be there in less than twenty minutes. He wants the book, so I need you to move it and hide it—"

"Nara—"

"Don't tell me where," I cut him off and yank my coat from the rack. "That way I won't be lying when I tell him where it is."

"Don't you dare go alone. Wait for me!"

"This is my Gran, Ethan," I say, tears filling my eyes. I grab my keys and head for the door. "It'll take me the full twenty minutes to get there. I can't wait. I have to save her if I can."

I hang up on him before he can say anything else and rush out the door.

My tires screech as I barrel into Westminster's parking lot in a record seventeen minutes. I don't even bother with the front desk. I quickly bypass it and head for the bathroom right off the lobby instead. I wait anxiously for the shuffling group of retirees to finally make their way toward the elevators, and then I slip out of the bathroom and blend in with the crowd.

I knock once on Gran's door. When Gran's sweet voice calls, "Come in, Nara," behind the wood, my stomach churns with nausea. I wipe my sweaty palms on my jeans, take a deep breath, then open the door.

The second I walk in, my heart jerks. Gran is standing to the left of the couch, rocking on her heels, a satisfied smile on her face. Clara's laying down with her eyes closed, fully stretched out on the sofa. The whole set up looks very wrong. I rush toward the sofa and fall to my knees beside Clara, hoping to see her chest rising and falling. When I don't detect anything, my heart jerks. Maybe she's in a deep sleep. God, please let that be the case.

"I got here in the time frame you gave me. What happened? Did you knock her out?" I ask calmly, while I'm freaking out on the inside.

Gran waves toward Clara like she's a piece of trash not worth her time. "She got on my nerves, so I killed her."

I open my mouth to speak, but nothing comes out. I'm just so devastated that an old woman's life is worth so little to this vile creature.

"What?" Gran shrugs at my look of horror. "I had to hitch a ride on the Clara train to get Gran to take off her broach, but then Clara freaked out once I hopped off. Her squawking did me in. Be glad I smothered her. I really wanted to rip her throat out." Her eyes narrow on my empty hands. "Where's the book?"

I stand on shaky legs and move closer to Gran, addressing the demon inside her. "It's somewhere safe."

Gran takes a step back, wary. "I told you to bring it here," the demon hisses.

I jerk my chin up. "And I need a guarantee that you won't kill my Gran once I tell you where it is."

"Do you really think I'm falling for that again?" the demon says, snorting.

My balled fists shake by my side, but I speak with conviction. "I was there when you double-crossed Danielle. And you killed Clara despite me meeting the deadline you gave me, yet you're calling me untrustworthy?"

Annoyance crosses Gran's face. "It took me a while. Lots of time and patience watching from a distance and waiting for just the right incentive. Then sweet old Gran shows up for Christmas. I can tell how much this old bat means to you." The demon snaps Gran's dentures twice, then taunts, "I can't believe you're going to let her die."

"No!" I rush up to Gran and press my hand to her chest, yelling, "Get out. Get the hell out of her!"

My body shudders and my chest feels tight like it did with David, but the demon in Gran only shakes her gray head, groggy for a second. Shoving me off Gran, he says, "What are you doing? Do you think you can expel me from her?"

Before I can respond, he sneers at me and grabs Gran's left hand, jerking it downward. The sound of snapping bone makes my stomach heave.

Swallowing my nausea, I step forward, hand raised, my chest aching. "No, please, no!" I beg the demon. "I would never risk Gran. The book is buried in the Oak Lawn Cemetery graveyard on the right side of Frederick Holtzman's gravestone."

The demon rolls Gran's head from one shoulder to another, then reaches for Gran's left forearm next. Leveling hateful eyes on me, he says, "You'd better not be lying or I'll yank her whole arm off next."

My heart jerks when he lifts Gran's frail arm and her hand dangles limply. "I promise!" I sob. "That's where I buried it. I'm not lying."

"Better move fast." Gran lets out an evil laugh, then her head lolls back and her body starts to fall.

I catch Gran before she hits the floor, but my shaking legs won't hold us, and we slowly sink to the floor together. Gran starts to moan, then quake all over. I'm so terrified for her, I just hold her close. I don't know what else to do.

"Nara!" Ethan opens the door at the same time my Gran goes very still.

"Help me, Ethan. She's not...oh, God...she's barely breathing!"

Before he can take two steps into the room, my father walks through the doorway behind him, police and para-medics in tow.

Pandemonium ensues around me. Police asking ques-tions. My father taking control of everything. I feel like I'm dreaming while the paramedics work on Gran, trying to get her vitals leveled out.

Ethan had moved to the doorway, staying out of the way. I glance at him a couple of times, but I don't really see him. I'm just so worried about Gran. They keep taking her pulse and calling out numbers that sound incredibly low, worried looks on their faces.

I know they're doing everything they can, but I still just want to scream, "Help her!"

ETHAN

My heart aches as I watch Nara sitting with her legs tucked under her on the floor next to her great aunt. She's trembling and looks so pale. I tried to go to her, but her father showed up with the paramedics and police, and they pretty much pushed me out of her Gran's apartment. So I hover in the doorway, hoping Nara will look my way again and see my sympathy and regret for what's happened.

All because of me. Of the secret she was trying to protect.

But she doesn't look my way, not really. I wait. I'm patient. I want her to know I'm here.

Her father steps in front of me, blocking Nara from my line of sight. "I think you should go. You've done enough."

"Excuse me, sir?"

He looks behind him at the policeman who's walking over to talk to Nara and shoves something in my hand. "I found this jammed in that dead woman's chest."

As I glance down at the Corvus broach I'd given Nara to give to her Gran, her father's voice moves closer and he grates in my ear, "I don't know what kind of dangerous shit you're part of, but I don't want my daughter mixed up in it. Take that with you. I know it's yours, and I don't want it traced back to Inara."

When he straightens, worry rages, but I remain calm. "Traced back? I don't understand."

His gaze slits and he pulls me out into the hall away from the door. "I knew something was off with you, so when I couldn't find that raven symbol anywhere on the web, I used my contacts and went to the police station to look through their database of gang related symbols and tattoos. The last thing I expected was to run across this same raven symbol listed in a recent unsolved murder."

I frown and shake my head. "What murder? I don't know what you're talking about."

"Someone had tagged the cement with that symbol not far from where they found the drowned body of a teenage girl named Harper Dabney. The police also found demon worship stuff at her house, so they think her death was some kind of sacrifice. The girl went to your school. Does the name Harper ring any bells?"

Shit, Harper. The demon that killed Harper must've left the symbol behind out of spite. I don't let the recognition show on my face. "No, it doesn't. I don't know anything about a murder. That symbol *is* one for protection, not demon worshiping, sir."

Mr. Collins shakes his head in a fast jerk. He doesn't believe a word I'm saying. "I don't know what Inferi are—" he pauses when my gaze hardens. I know Nara never told him the name Inferi.

Her father folds his arms, a stubborn look on his face. "Once I saw the partial sword tattoo on your back, I cloned Nara's phone. I heard her conversation with you earlier. That's how the police, ambulance, and I got here when you did. It's also how I know Corda's life was threatened over some damned book."

I'm amazed at how calm I'm remaining in the face of her father's fury. I can feel the Corvus in me pacing and seething. "I'd like to speak to Nara when she's able to talk."

"Do you want Inara to be next?" Brackets of anger form around his mouth, his tone low but furious. "I want you to stay the hell away from my daughter. Don't make me file a restraining order. You know I've got the connections to make it stick."

Her father turns away and walks back into the room to talk to the police. I move to the doorway and scan over the paramedics still working on her great aunt, and then to Nara, who looks like she's about to collapse as she watches the medical team buzzing all around.

Tell him to fuck off. Go in there! The Corvus pushes my foot forward. He wants me to rail at her father and defend myself, but I grab the doorjamb and stay firmly in place. It won't matter if I tell him the truth.

I never went to the graveyard. I came straight here. By now the demon has the book. He got what he wants and now Nara will finally be safe. No more demons will be hunting her or stalking her family. She has a clean slate. I can give her that at least.

I stare at her fingers clutched together. As far as I'm concerned, Nara did the job Michael expected of her. She convinced me that the Master Corvus has forgotten who he is, and now it's up to me to make sure he remembers.

I want to walk in there and hold her, to kiss her one last time and say goodbye, but maybe it's best this way.

You can't leave her. You must stay. She is everything to you.

She is everything. I love her enough to stop being so selfish. I feel my body tensing; I can sense the Corvus trying to control me and push me forward, but I lock my jaw and hold steady.

I won't leave her! he thunders in my head.

My gut clenches. He just said *I*. I'd been right to worry. My Corvus has attached to Nara. *And now you can't put her in danger anymore either, Corvus.*

No! You can't do this. She is so rare. You can't walk away!

You chose this vessel. Get used to it!

While I look at Nara one last time, hoping to soak in her features and commit them to memory, one of the paramedics says to the other, "Her heart has stopped. Get the defibrillator."

"I'm so sorry, Nara. For everything," I say quietly.

NARA

When the redheaded paramedic grabs the defibrillator, my thumping heart jumps into overdrive and tears roll down my cheeks. Why couldn't I expel that demon? Why could I save David, but not Gran?

While the machine makes its high-pitched charging sound, I dig my fingers into my thighs and glance to the doorway for Ethan, seeing him for the first time. His face is tense, his hand clenched on the doorjamb. He looks as worried as I feel.

My father squeezes my shoulder and says, "You have to be strong, Nari." His touch distracts me, drawing my attention to Gran once more. When Gran's body jerks with the defibrillator's shock, I swallow a sob and look back for Ethan, hoping for a signal from him that the book is safe. That he'll confirm that Clara's sacrifice and my Gran's life draining before my eyes aren't for nothing.

But he's gone.

**Thank you for following Ethan and Nara's journey.
Book 5, Awaken, is now available!**

If you found DESIRE an entertaining and enjoyable read, I hope you'll consider taking the time to leave a review and share your thoughts in the online bookstore where you purchased it. Your review could be the one to help another reader decide to read the BRIGHTEST KIND OF DARKNESS Series!

To keep up-to-date when the next P.T. Michelle book will release, join my free newsletter http://bit.ly/11tqAQN

OTHER BOOKS BY P.T. MICHELLE

In the Shadows
(Contemporary Romance, 18+)
Mister Black (Book 1 - Talia & Sebastian, novella, Part 1)
Scarlett Red (Book 2 - Talia & Sebastian, novel, Part 2)
Blackest Red (Book 3 - Talia & Sebastian, novel Part 3)
Gold Shimmer (Book 4 - Cass & Calder, novel, Part 1)
Steel Rush (Book 5 - Cass & Calder, novel, Part 2)
Black Platinum (Book 6 - Talia & Sebastian, stand alone)
Reddest Black (Book 7 - Talia & Sebastian, stand alone)
Blood Rose (Book 8 - Cass & Calder, stand alone) - Coming
June 2018

Brightest Kind of Darkness Series
(YA/New Adult Paranormal Romance, 16+)
Ethan (Prequel)
Brightest Kind of Darkness (Book 1)
Lucid (Book 2)
Destiny (Book 3)
Desire (Book 4)
Awaken (Book 5)

Other works by P.T. Michelle writing as Patrice Michelle

Bad in Boots series
(Contemporary Romance, 18+)

Harm's Hunger
Ty's Temptation
Colt's Choice
Josh's Justice

**Kendrian Vampires series
(Paranormal Romance, 18+)**
A Taste for Passion
A Taste for Revenge
A Taste for Control

Stay up-to-date on her latest releases:

Join P.T's Newsletter:
http://bit.ly/11tqAQN

Visit P.T. :
Website: http://www.ptmichelle.com
Twitter: https://twitter.com/PT_Michelle
Facebook: https://www.facebook.com/PTMichelleAuthor
Instagram: http://instagram.com/p.t.michelle
Goodreads:
http://www.goodreads.com/author/show/4862274.P_T_M
ichelle

P.T. Michelle's Facebook Readers' Group:
https://www.facebook.com/groups/PTMichelleReadersGr
oup/

ACKNOWLEDGEMENTS

To my awesome beta readers: Joey Berube, Amy Bensette, and Magen Chambers, thank you so much for reading *Desire* and giving honest and helpful feedback. You all have helped make *Desire* an even better story.

To my fabulous critique partner, Trisha Wolfe, thank you for reading *Desire* in record time and for your invaluable critiques. This book wouldn't be near as polished without you.

To my family, thank you for understanding the time and effort each book takes. I love you all for your wonderful support.

To the fans of the BRIGHTEST KIND OF DARKNESS series. Thank you for loving Ethan and Nara's story and for spreading the word about the books. I appreciate all your support.

ABOUT THE AUTHOR

P.T. Michelle is the *NEW YORK TIMES, USA TODAY*, and international bestselling author of the New Adult contemporary romance series IN THE SHADOWS, the YA / New Adult crossover series BRIGHTEST KIND OF DARKNESS, and the romance series: BAD IN BOOTS, KENDRIAN VAMPIRES and SCIONS (listed under Patrice Michelle). She keeps a spiral notepad with her at all times, even on her nightstand. When P.T. isn't writing, she can usually be found reading or taking pictures of landscapes, sunsets and anything beautiful or odd in nature.

To learn when the next P.T. Michelle book will release, join her free newsletter http://bit.ly/11tqAQN

Follow P.T. Michelle
www.ptmichelle.com

facebook.com/PTMichelleAuthor

twitter.com/PT_Michelle

instagram.com/p.t.michelle

youtube.com/PTMichelleAuthor

Printed in Great Britain
by Amazon